DRAGON SEEKING

DRAGON SEEKING
DRAGON APPARENT™ BOOK TWO

TALIA BECKETT

DISRUPTIVE IMAGINATION

This book is a work of fiction. All of the characters, organizations, and events portrayed in this novel are either products of the author's imagination or are used fictitiously. Sometimes both.

Copyright © 2020-2022 Talia Beckett
Cover by Bandrei
Cover copyright © LMBPN Publishing

LMBPN Publishing supports the right to free expression and the value of copyright. The purpose of copyright is to encourage writers and artists to produce the creative works that enrich our culture.

The distribution of this book without permission is a theft of the author's intellectual property. If you would like permission to use material from the book (other than for review purposes), please contact support@lmbpn.com. Thank you for your support of the author's rights.

LMBPN Publishing
PMB 196, 2540 South Maryland Pkwy
Las Vegas, NV 89109

Version 1.00 November, 2022
eBook ISBN: 979-8-88541-777-8
Print ISBN: 979-8-88541-975-8

To David. You're my favorite person to talk plot with. You get my genre, style and what I need to add to my books to make them work even better than my initial ideas. I hope we can always talk stories.

— Talia

THE DRAGON SEEKING TEAM

Thanks to the JIT Team:

Dorothy Lloyd
Diane L. Smith
Christopher Gilliard
Jan Hunnicutt
Jackey Hankard-Brodie
Paul Westman
Zacc Pelter

If I've missed anyone, please let me know!

CHAPTER ONE

The waves crashed around the base of the tower as I landed on the rope bridge, transforming back into a human as I did. For a moment, I paused, nervous about Ben's perception of my flight. Then I strode through the front door of the apartment.

"You're getting a lot better," he said as he barely looked up from the journal and notes long enough to acknowledge that I was even there. I fought the irritation that rose in me but couldn't help rolling my eyes anyway.

I was a red dragon. A red dragon called Scarlet. It had taken some time to get used to—it wasn't something I had grown up with. And I don't mean Scarlet being my name. I hadn't known I was a red dragon until two weeks ago.

That wasn't something to be proud of in the dragon world, however. No one wanted to be judged, picked on, or bullied, and that was exactly what had happened every day since living in the great dragon city.

I was the wrong color.

Mostly, I tried not to let it get to me, but occasionally it made me snappy, and Ben often bore the brunt of that.

"Any more progress?" I asked, knowing that the answer was probably no but unable to help but ask.

"Actually, there might be," he said. "But we need to be careful."

Taking this as my cue, I came into the main room to make sure I had heard him correctly. He was sitting at a small table with several books, a copy of the journal he was working with, his translated text, and an array of notes that covered the area.

I pulled up another chair, wanting to know what he'd discovered, and leaned in to read some of the notes. They talked of meeting a contact. Someone who had more information on me and knew where I might have come from.

My mouth fell open as I read and realized that Anthony had been doing more than protecting me. He'd been trying to find out more about me and my past—the source of my finances and why no one seemed to know where I'd been born or who my parents had been. There was little mention of me being a dragon, though he did express concern that he didn't want anyone to know who I was and what I might be.

There were several pages leading up to some kind of meeting place that was vaguely described, and then we ran out of text to translate again.

"How did you translate all this?" I asked.

"There was another phrase that I thought of when I opened the chest. Nothing inside that seemed to be important or relevant. Just some of the things I kept to remind me of events in my past. But I went to look inside again, and it reminded me of something he used to say to me whenever I put a new object inside."

Ben didn't elaborate on the "something," and I decided not to pry. Whatever it was, if he wanted me to know, he'd tell me. And as long as we were translating more of the journal, I didn't mind how we were doing it.

We'd found Anthony's journal hidden in his apartment when he had gone missing. It hadn't been readable because Anthony had written it in the ancient dragon language and in code. A different word translated each individual page, and it was based on phrases that he'd said to both Ben and me.

"This is...strange." Ben put down his pen.

I leaned closer, not sure what he meant. I mean, a lot of it was strange on some level. A guy who was totally unrelated to me was looking into my past because someone also entirely unrelated to me had told him to protect me. That was strange. It was strange that no one knew who my parents were. That all the red dragons who could have sired me were meant to be long dead by the time I was born was strange. That I was a *dragon* was strange.

As far as bizarre went, it wasn't that crazy that Anthony had found someone to talk to about me. It wasn't normal, but it was one of the more understandable actions.

Ben continued reading and didn't explain for a few minutes. Eventually, he sat back and looked at me.

"What have you learned so far about the shadow catchers and whom they report to?" he asked after studying me for a few seconds.

"That there's some evil demon thing locked in a gate, and dragons guard it. Which is why dragons hid from humanity when humanity was trying to kill you all. So that there would be dragons left to guard this gate."

"That's the very simple version of it, but yes. There's an evil locked beneath the earth, held there by the life force of the dragons in the world. If we live, it stays locked away. But it's not…dormant."

"The demon thing does stuff?"

"Sort of. It can communicate with those who are… unable to resist. And there are demons living in secret among humanity. These could shape-change and command the shadow catchers. If the rumors are to be believed, anyway. I've never come across anything but the odd shadow catcher. And honestly, until last week, only ever one at once."

"So four is extreme."

"Four is…insane. But remember, we only told the city council that there were three, and only briefly. Also that they were more interested in Anthony than anything else."

"Which is a complete lie."

"Do you want everyone grilling you every five minutes about why the shadow catchers are after you?"

I shook my head. There was no way I wanted that at all. I had already been subjected to all sorts of questions since I'd been back. It wasn't easy being a red dragon in this city. Already I had to be careful how I got to some lessons, and when and where I flew.

Some of the rumors of what had happened when we'd gone out to get Anthony and needed to set off a rescue orb had made a few dragons back off, but it was clear that I wasn't going to integrate easily into the community here.

In a lot of ways that wasn't anything new, however. I hadn't integrated particularly well into any society before.

My life had been one of an outcast or different or weird the whole way through. This was also nothing new. And I didn't see any point in complaining about it. It would get easier with time. It always did.

But none of that mattered now we'd found a lead.

"What does all this have to do with Anthony?" I asked.

"Well, it's complicated, but his journal talks about trying to prevent the demon from getting out and, well, something to do with an organization that we call a terrorist group."

"The dragon community has a terrorist group?"

"Yes. Sadly. They are actively working against the cities full of dragons that we have around the world and making it much harder on everyone, and there's been very little we could do about it in the past. For the most part, they're exiles, and anyone in the cities knows better than to have anything to do with them."

"But Anthony was talking to them?"

"Anthony mentions them. That's very, very different on a lot of levels." Ben exhaled and looked at the notes again.

"You think he was trying to protect me from them?" It seemed like we'd discovered yet another threat instead of something helpful.

"Maybe. I don't know, and I can't say for sure. I really hope not. But there's a chance, yes."

"That's not really a lead." I frowned and sat back.

"Actually, it might be."

Although I opened my mouth to demand that Ben

explain, I stopped as I noticed him shuffling the notes around until he'd found a piece of paper.

"We know that Anthony was looking for more information about something. And we know that he looked in all sorts of places. Even if this organization is a terrorist group, it seemed for a short while that Anthony might have worked with them to find what he needed, and if so, he didn't think they threatened you enough not to take that risk."

It was an odd sort of logic, but hearing Ben's views calmed my racing heart a little.

"So, you think we should go and look for the contact he had and find out what they told him?"

"Maybe. But this section cuts off in the middle. I think there's more to translate before we can do anything. At least, I'd like to try to find the next section. It's probably something you need to get the answer to, though. For the most part, they've been going back and forth between us."

I exhaled again, feeling more stressed than when I'd walked in. My shoulders were tense, and my heart ached, remembering that Anthony was gone. This wasn't the life I'd wanted to lead. I didn't want to be part of any kind of conspiracy or connected to anything like this. But then, none of my life had exactly gone to plan so far.

"Sounds like you're saying I'd best get back to lessons and what I've known all along and keep trying to think of words or phrases we can try next."

"Sorry, Red."

I rolled my eyes. Ben knew I didn't particularly like being called that. But there was also something about the way he said it. It held a sort of affection. We'd been thrown together by circumstance, and Ben wasn't the sort of person I would have chosen to have in my life at first glance, but he was the person Anthony had cared about and trusted enough to place him in my path.

The two of them had been together before Anthony had left the dragon city to protect me. When Anthony had gone missing, and Ben and I had both been thrown into a tailspin, the journal Anthony had left behind to guide us had made it clear that we were meant to be helping each other. And so far, it was also all in a code that we had to work together to translate.

It hadn't made a friendship any easier to forge in some ways, but it had shown us that we could rely on and trust each other, and that was enough.

"I think there's more to learn before we get in contact, but I'm going to do what I can to get to the bottom of it. But, Scarlet...My last translation phrase for the journal was very...personal. I think whatever your next one is... It might not be one you want to speak aloud, either. If that's true, I'd understand if you didn't want to write it down or if you wanted to try to translate it yourself. I can teach you."

"You've already tried to teach me how to do this, remember?" I replied, getting up again, unsure of what I would ever be embarrassed to say in front of Ben.

"I did. And I know it didn't go well. But...the option's there." He got to his feet as well, making it clear it was time for me to go and get back to my lessons.

I reached out and hugged him before he could do or say anything else. He was trying his best to help me, and his small house was the one place I felt safe in the entire city.

The council had agreed to assign me a small room below him, but it wasn't connected via any private route, and it was a single room that didn't really lock properly.

There was nothing that felt safe about it. Of course, I couldn't stay in Ben's room all the time either. There were lessons. And they weren't all bad. I was learning a bunch. And I had my favorite next—flying lessons. My excuse to let go and glide.

Leaving Ben to do whatever he did when he wasn't translating journal pages or talking to me, I made my way out of the apartment and went to one of the many rope bridges and walkways that connected all the towers in this dragon city.

I grinned as I looked around, always awed by the structures. Every building in the city was a tower. Many bridges connected them all, and dragons flew here, there, and everywhere. Each tower was unique and beautiful and carved from the same rock as the cliff the city was built on. It was surrounded by sea on every side, and the only exception was a narrow road that led to the nearby cliff. Humanity couldn't see anything beyond the cliff.

The flying lessons were conducted from the top of the tallest tower in the city. It was one of the few places where the teacher had assured me I was completely safe if I was standing on top of it, and the guards that lingered nearby had reinforced that promise on more than one occasion.

That hadn't stopped several dragons from trying to hamper my flying, especially when they saw me in dragon form, but there were always guards to see them off, and the teacher himself as well.

Of course, it wasn't easy for a teacher to teach when he

had to protect a student. And that meant I'd been quickly pulled out of the class I had been in, and now I had private lessons. Well, sort of.

I was only a few floors up, considering transforming to my dragon form and flying up, when a familiar dragon landed on the bridge in front of me, taking human form with style so he landed on human feet and his scales faded before my eyes.

"Scarlet, ready to fly?" he asked as he stepped to one side to let me pass.

Smiling, I nodded, always impressed by how Flick could fly and transform. I'd been much more wary of doing so since Ben had told me that if I changed into a dragon or human too close to other objects, I might form *around* them, and they could interfere with the body. We'd been in a forest at the time, and he'd been discouraging me from turning somewhere where I was guaranteed to end up with leaves and branches inside me.

Flick was one of the most skilled in the city at both flying and transforming. Or so I'd heard. And he liked to show off a little. He'd also chosen to embrace me as a friend, and I was lacking those. So I appreciated the gesture, if nothing else. He had taken a special interest in my flying lessons, and while he couldn't be at all of them, he made them an awful lot easier than they had been before he started coming along.

We were almost all the way to the top of the tower, the dragon willing to walk me up since I didn't dare fly, when I heard the familiar walk of another dragon. Neritas came around the corner, clad as always in a long black leather coat that appeared to float just above his large-booted feet.

For a moment, Neritas and Flick seemed to lock eyes. I always had this slight expectation that they were going to start a fight or try to murder each other with looks, but every time so far, they'd only given each other a brief nod and then focused on me. It was an almost bizarre unspoken gentleman's agreement that nothing would happen while I was around.

"Red," Neritas said. "Want to get a little air? The old fella's waiting for you."

I nodded, aware that I was probably a little late. I was often late for lessons. Everyone else flew to their lesson in the tower after the first couple of weeks, but I still wasn't, and it was starting to get to me already. I wasn't anywhere near as safe flying anywhere else in the city, even with my two masculine escorts and the respect they seemed to command. As such, I only flew short hops when I was being watched by Neritas and Flick or needed to get a very short distance alone.

That meant my legs were getting a serious workout with each day I lived in the city. There were always so many stairs to climb. I needed to get better at flying so I could outrun all the dragons giving me a hard time like Flick could.

CHAPTER TWO

"Ah, Scarlet, there you are," my teacher, Jared, said as soon as I appeared.

I always expected to notice some frustration when I walked up onto the roof of the tower with my two accompanying dragons, but he only ever smiled and motioned for me to come closer.

This time was no different.

"You've been making such good progress, and since you have two wonderful role models with you, I wanted to try something harder today. Are you up for that?" he asked as the sky behind him shone with the brightness of the sinking sun and the clouds building on the horizon. They looked dark, and I knew they hadn't been there before, but no one else seemed worried about them.

"Whatever you think is best," I replied. I loved flying, and I was aware that everything I could learn might keep me from getting bullied one day, assuming it didn't give me anything else to be bullied over. It might even save my life if the rumors of what happened to red dragons were true.

"Fantastic. I thought you'd be willing to try. You've got the guts a real flier needs." He clapped his hands together, and his smile got wider. "Right, form up and into the air. We'll start hovering above the tower. You'll have me, our usual two black guards, and your friends around you, with you in the middle. Then I'm going to lead the way, and they'll stay in formation around you and come too. I know everyone else can handle this and should enjoy it, so we'll just go for it, and if we need to rescue you, you'll be in good hands."

I raised an eyebrow at his last sentence, but I wasn't sure I could argue with it. Rescue me? That was a new prospect that hadn't entered my thoughts. I mean, there had been a few times when he had to come to my rescue, but only to deter other dragons from getting in my way.

Despite my slight misgivings and the strangeness of his words, I did as suggested and finally morphed into my dragon form. It always felt strange at first. I didn't feel any different, but my vision shifted, and I could look down and see the red-scaled limbs and peek around to see my wings.

I rose into the sky and gently flapped my powerful wings up and down to keep myself at roughly the same height. As soon as they saw me, two guards leaped up from nearby towers and came to flank me from the rear, and both of my friends took up positions in front of me on my left and right.

The teacher took his position directly in front of me for now, the only one facing us as the rest of us faced him. It was how we'd all flown many times—a formation I was always entirely grateful for. Between us, we had almost every color going. Our teacher was a pearl white, my friends yellow and green, and with me red and the two guards black, it was an almost perfect grouping. We were only missing the beautiful blue dragons that were also about in the city.

Of course, there was a good chance we'd attract the attention of plenty of other dragons soon. There were always a few who came to watch, though they didn't dare to interfere anymore. And I often noticed some of the older dragons hanging back near the council building.

It wasn't the nicest way to learn to do something that could have disastrous results if done wrong, with so many watching and possibly judging me, but so far, I hadn't made a fool of myself.

There was always the fear that this was going to be the first time, however, and that fear really didn't ever seem to go away. Who knew what would happen today?

Right, can you hear me, everyone? my teacher asked in my head, and probably everyone else's. It was one of the benefits of being in dragon form—we could all telepathically link.

The hardest part of that had been learning to keep everyone else out and make the words I was thinking appear in other dragons' heads. There had been times I had responded, and no one had heard me. Not ideal at all, really, but I was sorted on that now, for the most part.

With other dragons around trying to distract me by projecting thoughts into my head, one of the first things Neritas had done was pull me aside, find us a place to take dragon form indoors, and teach me to guard my mind. I had been eternally grateful to him ever since.

Now I heard my teacher and the other four gently responding, and I added my own voice to it.

Perfect. Then let's begin. We're going straight up, and we're not stopping. As he spoke, he powered upward and kept going, making me almost panic that I was going to be left behind, but I found my body responding instinctively. He'd been training me in strange ways, and I was having two lessons every day, for now, to try to catch me up to other dragons my age.

Thankfully, it meant my dragon form responded to the demand he was placing on it, and I quickly caught up with him. He didn't stop accelerating, climbing higher and going faster and faster.

I fought to do the same, knowing I was meant to be copying him, and both Flick and Neritas were easily keeping up, matching the acceleration. I tucked my feet back and tried to make myself streamlined, inhaling with each downbeat as I'd been instructed when getting higher as fast as possible. It wasn't the easiest way to fly.

With each downbeat that propelled us higher and higher, and every little bit of extra speed we eked out of our bodies, I expected to get left behind or to see our teacher do something else, but he just kept going, and I had to keep following.

We were leaving the city far behind yet staying in the strange forcefield that kept us safe in the hidden city. The sky got brighter with the sun more visible this far up, but it also got colder, and I was soon shivering and thinking that I was going to freeze. Ben's blue dragon ability to make himself warmer would be useful about now.

Instead, I had to carry on flying as my teacher continued. We rose even higher, and I started to feel faint. The air I was breathing was not sustaining the attempt to fly.

Okay, slow now. We're almost at the maximum. Slow your breathing and glide up the rest of the way.

Grateful, I let my exhausted wings rest and tucked them in against my body again. It was beautiful to just let my momentum carry me higher as the world got darker and the stars started to shine above.

I felt my head going fuzzy as the lack of oxygen started to affect me. Not sure what to do, I looked for my teacher, but he was gliding ahead, seeming to level off.

What now? I asked, not completely sure I projected the thought well enough, but he turned himself around.

Fuzzy head? He studied me.

I tried to nod, but it made my vision darken. I wasn't sure what was happening, and my body seemed unable to respond.

It's okay. Stop trying to breathe fast. Just let it wash over you, embrace the cold, listen to my voice, and slow and calm your body down. The human part of you wants to breathe harder and faster to get enough oxygen. But the dragon part of you can handle this with no trouble. Let it.

I blinked, not sure what he could mean as I tried to gulp down enough oxygen.

Calm, Ben's voice was suddenly in my head too. *Just be calm. You've got this. I know you do.*

But I didn't, and before I knew it, my vision was going black and the stars seemed to be fading away again. Cold rushed past me, making me feel even more frozen, and I had to fight the shivers my body wanted to give in to.

You're a dragon. Remember that. Think. Control yourself.

Ben didn't stop talking, his words calm. I heard my teacher's along with it, but other voices soon crowded in around it. So many, and many of them saying unkind things I couldn't entirely process.

Breathe, Ben commanded.

The word cut through all the others, far louder, and I did as he suggested, sucking in loads of oxygen and air and clearing my head as I did. Only then did I realize that I was falling, but the dragons who had flown up with me were still floating down, not leaving my side.

For a moment, I continued to panic, but another easier lungful of air and the ability to shut out all the unhelpful voices from all the other hangers-on flying up to meet us made me calmer again.

Within another couple of seconds, I slowed myself and paused in the air, with the teacher in front of me again and everyone around me.

I didn't think or say anything as I hovered again, way above the city and clouds, the dark horizon that had loomed at the beginning of the lesson now a storm that almost entirely obscured the city.

That was... The teacher's thought trailed off.

Stupid, I finished for him. *I panicked and passed out.*

It was amazing, Neritas responded. *I've never seen anyone get that high that fast on their first attempt.*

First attempt? I asked, projecting the thought just to him.

Yeah. We've all practiced that a lot of times to be able to handle it. Everyone passes out the first time. Everyone. And most people have to be caught. You got all the way to the stars and then rescued yourself. And I bet you had the crowd of idiots below screaming insults in your head as you fell.

Something like that.

I took some more deep breaths. My body was still cold, but the sensation was somehow no longer as bad. What had just happened?

Switching my focus back to my teacher, I noticed he was smiling like a Cheshire cat. Had I really done well?

Come on, let's go back up, he said. *We'll go slower this time.*

I wanted to argue and tell him I wasn't ready for it, but I had a feeling I wasn't going to get away with arguing, and the rest of the dragons went that way, giving me little choice if I didn't want to lose my guard of honor.

This time we flew up gently, and he talked me through shallowing out my breathing and taking in enough air before I got too high for my dragon form to stop coping as well. It was one of the most amazing experiences as we went higher and I let the cold wash through me, my wings responding automatically to the air to keep me flying high.

It was as if the dragon form was designed for so much more than I'd realized. I had to just let it do what it wanted and stop getting in the way. But it was also so much more than that.

Thought and strategy had gone into getting the most out of what the dragon body was capable of. And the truth was that we were capable of great things. I also noticed that very few of the dragons who normally followed my flights had come up this high. Were they capable of this, or had I just found something that would enable me to get away from a lot of dragons who bothered me?

Most can't come up this high, Jared said as if he'd read the thought, although there was no way he could have.

I grinned and kept climbing, calmer than I had been in

a long time. I'd felt embarrassed at first, and I was pretty sure that I was going to be exhausted when I got back to the city, but this had been a lesson I needed.

We got to about the same height as before, and I wasn't pushed to go any higher. My dragon body coped better with it this time compared to my first attempt. There were just the six of us up this high, and I paused to simply look around.

So much of the earth was visible that the curve of its surface was noticeable. Lights were coming on in cities that were losing the light of the sun. Our dragon city was entirely under clouds as a small storm settled over it.

Watching the storm, I seemed to go into a sort of trance, until I heard my teacher chuckle.

You would skip ahead to the next part of the lesson and work out how to get your body into a hibernation state in the air without being taught, wouldn't you? he asked when I looked at him.

I wasn't sure what he meant at first, but I felt the difference in my body. My heart rate was slower than it had ever been, and I couldn't focus properly. Everything seemed to be happening at a different speed, but there was also something calming and amazing about it.

Having already taken a while to get up this high and then gone down and back up, learning a bunch on the way, my lesson was already drawing to an end. Encouraged by my teacher, we flew back down.

The storm did not look in the least inviting.

As we got closer to the dark clouds, the other dragons hanging in the sky above it and waiting for me came in closer than ever, and my four guards and teacher formed up tightly around me.

This might be a bit bumpy, my teacher warned as we got closer and closer to the swirling gray mass.

I wasn't entirely sure what he meant by that, but I suspected I wasn't going to get a chance to ask questions as the distance between us and the storm closed fast.

It obscured my vision almost immediately, and all I could do was keep flying down at the same rate. Somewhere inside this thing, the other dragons would be flying around, watching for me to screw up. There had been more than a handful of other dragons in the sky waiting for me. I would need to watch out for them as well, and not just my escorts.

I was partway through it before I realized I was drenched. And then lightning flashed, crackling over my scales and tingling in the strangest way. It lit up the inside of the storm, showing me the outlines of other dragons as they were also struck.

I marveled at the insanity of the last hour of my life. Here we were, flying through a thunderstorm without any fear or danger, yet a human would have been killed if they were hit the way we'd just been.

Before I could think any more about it, however, something hit me from behind, raking across the scales on my back. I roared in pain, surprising even myself.

They're attacking in the storm. Dive, Ben instructed, the ever-constant presence of my mentor a welcome one.

I did as he said, not sure I could do anything else. It would help protect my wings as well, something Ben had pointed out several days ago. Tucking them tightly into my body, I hurtled downward as fast as I could.

At the same time, I projected to Flick, Neritas, and Jared that I'd done so, knowing I might need their help as I came out the other side.

It seemed to take forever, but I eventually came out beneath the clouds. The city below me glowed and glittered with the lights of a thousand candles and lamps. The sight was beautiful, but it also showed me how alone I was. I'd gotten ahead of everyone else.

A moment later, I spotted a familiar large blue dragon leaping up from one of the towers and powering up in the air toward me. I continued to dive, helping to close the gap, not daring to look behind and see if there was anyone else to help.

Other dragons responded to my presence, many of them also familiar, but their presence far less than friendly. I had few allies in the air.

Ben roared louder than anything I'd ever heard, and I felt a bolt of heat shoot out from him in a cone around me, leaving me safe but warning anyone who got close to me that he would act aggressively.

It made several of the dragons hesitate, and then my two black dragon guards came down over me, and my teacher reappeared.

You're safe again, he said, his voice only giving away a trace of the anxiety he might have felt about what had just happened.

I exhaled and opened my wings again, slowing and aiming for the top of the tower I'd taken off from. With my back hurting and adrenaline pumping through my body, I landed and morphed back into a human.

Immediately I stumbled. Ben caught me, careful not to touch my back.

"This needs to stop," he said, almost growling the last word.

I nodded, clenching my fists and turning to look up at the sky full of dragons. There was no way to tell which one of them had hurt me, but I planned to find out, and I was going to make whoever it was regret it someday.

CHAPTER THREE

Wincing, I padded into Ben's room again. It was the day after my eventful flight, and Ben had insisted I sleep in his bed or somewhere he could keep an eye on me. Not that I'd slept very well. My entire back was bandaged up, and I'd needed several stitches.

It didn't seem fair that an injury I'd taken in dragon form had translated to my human form, but Ben had informed me that treating it in either form would carry over, and I'd heal swiftly just from being in the city with other dragons. Something about the magic in the air.

Grateful that was a thing somehow, I hadn't argued when he'd also insisted I stay close.

"All right. I think we need to translate some more of this journal and get you out of the city for a day or two. Let heads cool," he said as he came back inside as well.

"Why?" I asked, not sure where he'd been.

He tensed his jaw for a moment as if he was considering what to tell me and not sure he should say anything, but then he caught the expression on my face and exhaled. I folded my arms across my chest.

"Some of the dragons are claiming it was your fault. That they were trying to get through the storm and you were still half-conscious from the flight and crashed into them."

"But no one else is even hurt."

"No…but the council… There's a lot of bias against red dragons. Against you being hotheads and difficult to work with."

"Tell me again why I'm here."

"Because learning everything is good for you, if nothing else, and I can protect you here from them better than I can out there from the shadow catchers. I'm not Anthony."

I frowned, all the anger vanishing from me as Ben ran a hand through his hair and slumped into a chair. I didn't know what to say. He looked defeated, his face downcast as he shook his head.

"You're not Anthony. And we both miss him a lot, but he trusted you with whatever this is, just as he did me. We might not be him, either of us, but he clearly believed in both of us," I finally replied.

"Not enough to tell me all this while he was alive." The pain in Ben's voice was clear. His usual strength cracked under the last word, and his eyes shone with the threat of tears.

I moved to his side and put a hand on his shoulder, not sure what else to say. It hurt to lose a friend, and Anthony hadn't been gone that long. And he'd left behind him a lot of unresolved relationship issues. I would have given anything to have him back, but I couldn't do anything about it. All I could do was try to work out what he'd been trying to achieve and stick with Ben until we saw it through.

No sooner had I thought this than I remembered something Anthony used to say about the trouble with loving people.

Reaching for one of the pieces of paper scattered on Ben's desk, I shifted to look for a pen. Ben handed one to me, not needing me to say anything for him to know I'd had a brainwave.

Grinning, I wrote the phrase and put the pen down.

Love is like a fire, but you can never tell if it will burn down your house or warm it.

Ben chuckled and nodded.

"Yes. He said that to me a couple of times too. I don't doubt that's what we need next. Get comfortable. We're translating this now. Hopefully, it will give us what I need, 'cause it seems like he's still taking care of both of us from wherever he is now."

"He's somewhere better, and I'm sure he'll be pleased with what we're managing," I said as I perched on the end of the sofa, careful not to lean back.

I wasn't sure I believed my words, but Ben needed to hear them, and it felt good to say them either way.

For the next few minutes, there was nothing but the sound of Ben's pen scratching across the paper and the swish of pages as he flicked back and forth through the translation codex he'd copied.

I didn't interfere or offer to help and translate again. It wasn't worth it. My skills clearly lay in other things. Like flying and making a nuisance of myself.

I stifled a couple of yawns while I waited, not wanting to break Ben's concentration. I'd been in too much pain and annoyed at having to sleep in strange positions to rest well last night.

None of it seemed to pull Ben from his work, but the further he went, the less pleased he looked. Frown lines appeared on his face as he set his jaw.

By the time he was done, he was the angriest I'd ever seen him. He didn't say another word as he got up and walked to the window, rubbing a hand over his chin. I went to the journal and read the last bit he'd translated.

It's done. I've met with Jace again. She's one of the most capable dragons I've ever met in a pinch. And it's been a pleasure to work with one of her kind again. I still haven't told them anything about what I'm doing, but I'm earning their trust, and it helps that I haven't been back to Detaris in some time. They're less welcome there than I am.

Of course, they know that what they're doing makes it worth it, and I can see why they think that. It makes it easier to work with them, but it's not something I thought I'd be doing even a year ago. I often wonder what Ben would think. I know he wouldn't approve, but I hope he'd come to understand.

Still, they're helping me, and I'm helping them. It's enough for now. It has to be. None of us know how long this will last or if we can keep going. The council doesn't make any of it easy, and I'm starting to suspect they don't really want to.

I exhaled, getting the idea of what I'd just read.

"Tell me about this group of dragons," I said as Ben

turned back to me. "Who are they, and why are they something that Anthony was worried about?"

"They're terrorists, as I've already said. They've fought with the council on more than one occasion. They don't hide well enough, and they generally make life harder for all dragons everywhere. While they still try to operate in the shadows, they aren't staying out of the affairs of humanity, and some of them have even swayed the direction of wars and conflicts to better themselves in the past."

"But Anthony trusted these people with something. Or to help him in some way."

Ben frowned and looked at the journal.

"So it would seem. But I don't understand how he could have. He used to talk about how important it was to be honorable. To do the right thing even if it hurt sometimes. To not let the wrong thing happen out of habit or because we'd not questioned our beliefs. He wouldn't have been comfortable working with terrorists."

"And that leads to the possibility these dragons aren't as bad as they seem, not that Anthony did something out of character. That wasn't like him, so let's not assume he did it." I sat forward a little, feeling my heart rate pick up with the passion of my words. I didn't want to tell Ben what to think, but I also didn't know much about this terrorist group.

If there was a chance Anthony hadn't done something strange and they weren't as bad as people thought they might be, then I was going to give them the benefit of the doubt. It made more sense for me to doubt rumors, not Anthony, than it did for me to think of Anthony as being okay with working with terrorists.

"Okay. I have heard too much about this group to blindly trust that they're all good, but you have a point. And either way, this Jace person and how Anthony found her in LA is all we've got to go on. We should let you spend another day here, heal up, go to another lesson or two, and then we should go to LA for a few days and see what we can sort out."

"And the council will be okay with that?"

"I'll tell them that you need to cool down and need time away from dragons for a bit and that everything with Anthony is still getting to you, especially that we didn't find any reason for him to be in the woods."

I nodded as I got to my feet to go to my next set of lessons. Of course, we had found something, but we weren't telling the council about any of this. Whatever Anthony was protecting me from, it was better that no one knew about it. I hadn't understood at first why that was, but I was beginning to.

This wasn't a great place for me to be as a red dragon. But I had nowhere else to go. Only my friends from before were even bothering to check in on me, and their messages had already tapered off as I'd had to reply that I was busy more and more.

Not sure I wanted to go anywhere while I hurt so much, but feeling as if Ben had dismissed me with his last sentence and that he wanted the relatively harmless excuse to be alone for a while, I grabbed the tablet-like device I used for almost everything in the city, stuffed it in a bag along with a bottle of water and a snack bar, and made my way from the small apartment.

I hadn't gone more than a few bridges when Flick appeared and grinned at me.

"Need an escort to the next lesson?" he asked, and I almost burst into tears at him. The answer was an obvious yes. The pain was making me walk funny, and there was no way I dared to morph into a dragon, no matter what Ben had said about how it would still heal up just fine in my dragon form.

Flick put his arm gently around me and over my shoulders.

"It was a crappy thing for them to have done. I know they're all saying you started it, and I'm sorry this whole thing is proving really shitty for you, but it will stop. Something else will happen, and you won't be the new distraction from how trapped we all feel."

The last sentence took me by surprise—it hadn't occurred to me that they would be feeling just as stuck and caged as I did inside this small place. And for most of them, there was no leaving the city. Not really. And here I was, knowing that Ben was finding me all sorts of reasons to leave and I was going to get out for the third time already.

Many of the other dragons' actions made sense, but either way, I knew Flick was right. It would need to stop. But I wasn't sure it would do so without some encouragement from me. At least, not any time soon. There were simply too many reasons for them to continue focusing on me, even if something did change. And too few things that could happen to distract them in such a close and confined city.

Whatever happened, I was likely to have to solve my own problem, one way or another. I couldn't continue like this, and I couldn't rely on guys like Flick and Neritas, who probably had ulterior motives, to keep me safe forever.

For now, though, I let Flick keep his arm over my shoulders as he gently got me to my next lesson.

It was boring and I barely paid attention, but it gave Ben some time alone, and it gave me some time to process and heal.

When Flick invited me to get some lunch with him and made it obvious he expected me to say yes, I grew even more wary. Was I making it look too much like I was interested in him as more than a friend? I needed to understand what was going on in his head.

"What is it that no one likes about red dragons?" I asked once we were sitting down at a table out of the way and tucking into hamburgers with fries.

"You're hotheads. Or pretentious and arrogant. Or both. And born to royalty or something special. You have the most useless magical power of all of us, though, so it's not like there's anything to be pretentious about. Assuming the weird rumors aren't true."

"Rumors?" I asked, deciding not to respond to potentially being called arrogant and pretentious.

Being a hothead wasn't a new accusation or necessarily wrong. My temper got me into trouble sometimes.

"Yeah. Some say that the reason red dragons are royalty is because they can unite us in some way magically. Seems all they've ever done is divide us, though."

"Not all of them." Neritas sat down at a spare seat, forcing Flick to move over slightly. I wondered if I was going to end up pissing one of them off at some point, but Flick took it graciously and made space.

I waited for Neritas to explain, but he didn't right away.

"You think the red dragons can do cool stuff?" Flick asked a minute or so later, popping the question so I didn't have to.

"Yeah. Look at Scarlet. She's stronger, faster, and able to survive the shadow catchers better than anyone we know, and she hasn't even had a fraction of the lessons we've had. There's got to be something there. And I think Anthony knew it. Ben does too. Why else would a blue and a white dragon volunteer to protect a red and claim her as their own?"

"I'm sitting right here, you know," I said when Neritas had finished talking.

"Sorry, Scarlet, but it's all true. You have everyone being a dick to you because you're already better than most of them and you haven't had to study to get there. That you're red is just making it even more of a sting. No one likes folks who look like they have it easy."

"Yet both of you are willing to eat lunch with me and be there in my flying lessons. Why aren't you two treating me the way everyone else does? Or assuming that a life growing up in the human social system with no parents was easy on me? Or how being a social outcast in both the human world and the dragon one isn't a problem at all?"

"Because if any of those rumors are even slightly true, I don't want to piss off the only red dragon in this city. And besides. It's funny watching everyone else get their panties in a bundle over seeing me sit down with you," Neritas replied, refreshingly honest.

Flick looked as if he was thinking as he took another bite of his hamburger and chewed slowly.

"I think you looked so normal when you came in with Ben. And so genuinely awed by seeing the city, yet vulnerable, like it was all too much too soon, that I don't believe you can be anything but another person just like us. Someone who needs some friends and a new place to stay because the shadow catchers took away your old life. That, and you try hard. You might be red and special, but you're not expecting life to hand you everything on a silver platter."

It was one of the nicest ways that anyone had told me they didn't think badly of me, and coupled with the amusing response from Neritas, it made me feel a little better. At least I had two friends my own age in the city. And I had Ben, even if he wasn't the perfect role model.

CHAPTER FOUR

It seemed strange to be heading down to the lower levels of the city again, but Ben led the way. I walked alongside Flick, who had decided to see me off. It had taken another two days to convince the council to let me and Ben leave, and I was already hurting a lot less and able to move more.

Ben had still insisted that I sleep in his apartment, and I'd had Flick and Neritas escort me pretty much everywhere, but it was almost as if everything had gone back to normal—with the exception of no more flying lessons until I was better.

Already I missed it. There was something very freeing about flying, especially as a powerful dragon, high above an entire city. But it wasn't something I could do while hurting this much, and I got the impression that in response to the accusation that I had attacked someone while flying, the elders wanted me to stop doing so for a while.

Ben had been surprisingly tight-lipped about the elders and their response to everything that was going on, and I had been forced to carry on with lessons without my favorite one.

As we approached the small parking lot where authorized dragons could choose a car to drive, I noticed there were plenty of dragons milling around, and some of them appeared to be arguing.

"No. I know that computers are hard to understand, but you can't do that with them and get away with it. Let me…" The guard stopped when she saw me, and then she noticed Ben.

"Keep doing what you're doing," my mentor said to the guards. "I'm going to take the usual car and see us off to the usual place. Got to sort some stuff in the woods where we found Anthony, and we're going to take a day or two to be tourists in LA to let Scarlet pretend she's human again for a bit."

I wanted to roll my eyes and get annoyed at Ben's description of me, but it was our cover story. We couldn't exactly tell the guards on the city gate that we wanted to go contact a terrorist organization well known in the dragon world. I doubted any of them would understand.

It was especially difficult when I wasn't sure even Ben understood Anthony's motivation. But Anthony had liked them, and that was enough for me, for now. If they were who they said they were and not who the city thought they were, I was going to be fine with them. But Ben wasn't convinced, and I wasn't stupid enough to try to get him to see differently.

The guards waved us through, reminding me just how much clout my mentor had in the city. This wasn't a normal level. And I was getting the benefits.

Once Ben had unlocked the car, Flick placed my bag in the trunk, having carried it for me all the way down from Ben's apartment. For a few minutes, I'd expected him to run off with it, my past life experiences coming into play, but he hadn't, and I convinced myself to calm down and not keep expecting the worst.

"See you when you get back?" he asked, almost as if he wasn't sure I would.

"Yeah. Not sure exactly how long we'll be, but I'll message when I'm back if you don't see us come in," I replied, wondering where Neritas had got to. He hadn't said goodbye at all, and I wondered if I'd pissed him off or something.

Not wanting to make a protracted scene of leaving, I got into the passenger seat of the car before Ben had even stuffed his bag in the trunk beside mine, and then I sat back and closed my eyes as if I wanted to do nothing more than sleep.

It was antisocial of me, but there wasn't another part of me left to cope. My back didn't really hurt much anymore, but my emotions were still all over the place. And I didn't like not feeling in control.

Thankfully, Flick didn't appear offended and returned to the city proper by transforming and flying up. He was definitely still a show-off and did a few rolls in the air as he flew off. I grinned, despite trying to pretend I wasn't paying any attention to him.

I exhaled as Ben got in beside me.

"Ready?" he asked.

"As ready as anyone could be for the crazy life we've begun leading," I replied.

This earned me a small nod and Ben setting his jaw.

"What did you say to the elders to let me out so easily this time?" I asked when we were on the cliff road and out of the strange force field around the city that kept it hidden.

"I didn't have to say anything much. I think they remember what you did to the shadow catchers the first time we were out there, and how you walked out of the city to go back the day after and find out what Anthony had been trying to hide. Even if that doesn't help enough, they know there isn't a lot they can do to stop you and that you're a lot safer than most dragons in the city."

I exhaled, the words bringing back both painful and confusing memories. I had no clue how I had managed to hurt the shadow catchers when they had tried to attack us and hit the shields. But I had. Something Ben had thought impossible.

No one, including Ben, had brought it up since. We'd mostly agreed not to, and I thought that was a pretty good idea, but it was still not quite something I understood, and because I didn't understand it, it made it hard to feel comfortable doing it.

We drove for a while toward LA, both of us lost in thoughts. It seemed as if there was always a lot that went unspoken or ignored. Neither of us had brought up why the shadow catchers might have been after me or where they had gone. It wasn't a subject Ben seemed to like talking about.

On several occasions, I had wondered if it was all too painful for him. If it reminded him of Anthony. Or if he didn't actually like my company that much but put up with it because he felt as if he had to. I wasn't used to anyone liking me, and it had been strange to read praise for me in Anthony's translated journal.

Of course, there was also the occasional remark about Ben, but it wasn't as common. After all, it wasn't as if Anthony was trying to protect Ben, and they didn't seem to have seen each other much in the time Anthony had been watching over me.

As we got closer to LA, I found myself thinking more and more of the life I'd left behind there and what the other dragons thought of it. Everyone in Detaris was assuming that I wanted to be in their city from now on, but there had been parts of my old life that I liked.

There were friends that I'd left behind. And some of them had checked in on me over the last week. My boss might have fired me after only a few days, but friends had tried to make sure I was okay.

Thinking about them, I spent the next part of the journey messaging them and letting them know I was still alive, as well as asking about them and their worlds. I couldn't really say a lot—none of what I'd been through was something I could share—but I could ask them how they were and check in.

"You missing the folks back in the city already?" Ben asked.

"No. I don't know them that well. Or have either of their numbers," I replied, but my cheeks grew hotter despite my denial.

"Oh, so there's more than one dragon who has caught your eye."

"Not exactly. There are two who don't treat me like I'm

scum and are actually being nice. But I don't know exactly why, and neither is trying to do anything more than protect me, it seems. There's another dragon in my cooking class who is also nicer than the rest, but that's not saying much." I shrugged and tried to work out where this was going.

"Protecting you is a pretty big deal. It's not…easy always, being an ally to a red dragon."

"Neither of them seems to mind. I asked. I don't think anyone dares to give Neritas any trouble, and Flick seems to be able to outfly everyone."

"Just…be careful. They'll have their reasons, and we still don't know what Anthony was so worried about."

I nodded, not sure I wanted to talk about what their reasons might be. There was a danger this conversation was going to go toward talking about relationships and how the only two so-far-decent dragons might want sex. The talk every parental figure felt they had to give at some point. I was old enough to be legal, and sure I didn't want to discuss something like that with Ben, so it was time to change the topic of conversation.

"I was actually messaging my human friends," I told him. "The people I hung out with before I was forced to live in a dragon city. Believe it or not, I had a few. I was thinking it would be nice to see them if I get the chance."

This made Ben frown even more, and I wasn't sure if he was going to respond or grant me any kind of acknowledgment. I didn't know what the rules of Detaris were, but I knew that if I didn't see at least one of my old friends soon, they were going to worry.

The time had vanished in a haze of lessons, but it had

been almost three weeks since I had dropped everything and gotten in a car with Ben. It wasn't like me to avoid my friends for that long. And though no one was prying yet, it was clear they had questions and wanted to know where I had been and why I hadn't been responding very much.

"Some of them are around tomorrow evening, and they're having a get-together dinner. You don't have to come with me," I continued.

"No. Just no. I mean, I understand you wanting to see some friends of yours. But you have to know, Scarlet. You can't go back to your old life. Even if I thought it was okay for you to talk to them and not slip up, the dragon society is watching you right now. And on top of that, we still don't entirely know what's going on with you. You could put them in danger."

I frowned as I listened to Ben speak. I didn't care what the other dragons thought of me at all, but it bothered me that my actions might lead to any of my friends getting hurt.

"You miss them?" Ben asked when I still didn't reply.

"Yeah. They really do care about me."

"I'm sure they do. Despite that frosty exterior you have and the way you try to keep everyone out and not tell people what's going on in your head, you're a good person. I don't doubt that you matter to them."

Blinking, I tried to process what he'd said. Had he just complimented me? A dragon who had only taken me into his life because he had to and hadn't always appeared to be happy about it?

"I know it won't be easy, but it's probably best if you let them go entirely. You can't keep them in your life and not invite more trouble. I know you rebel. And I know that you don't like being told what to do. But you have to start a new life. Anthony should have never indulged everything the way he did with you before now."

I opened my mouth to argue with the last part, but I got the feeling that it would be a waste of breath. The truth was that his words stung, and I wasn't in the best place to hear someone telling me that I wasn't the person I should be. That I rebelled more than I should. I had tried to be more balanced after seeing some of the things other kids in the system had done just to be rebellious.

Putting my phone aside for now, I tried to think of something else. I wasn't sure what to do. Or what was best. But I knew that Ben was right about one thing—I couldn't put my old friends in danger. And I didn't know how safe I truly was.

No one knew. And that was even more worrying.

Not for the first time, it hit me hard how much I missed Anthony. He had been protecting me from a lot more than I'd realized.

CHAPTER FIVE

I got out of the car finally and stretched as I looked around the area of LA we'd stopped in. No matter what had happened, this city still felt like home more than any other had. Yet it was also strange. Something about it held the threat of the shadow catchers.

I'd been chased through the city one too many times to feel entirely at ease. Especially after they'd followed me to a forest to the north and killed my mentor and friend there.

Now I was back in the city to try to find out what else my mentor might have been protecting me from. And I only had Ben here to help me. It wasn't ideal.

"It's a real shame we don't have a black dragon with us," Ben said as he came around to my side of the car and pulled his phone out.

I didn't need him to explain. The last time we'd faced shadow catchers, I had somehow combined my powers with those of Ben and the black dragon trying to help us. It had resulted in a strange power shield that had not only repelled the vile creatures of the night but also hurt them.

Although I had no idea exactly what I'd done, I was pretty sure I could have replicated it if I needed to. It was a thought that no doubt brought Ben comfort as well as me.

"Where do we need to go?" I replied instead.

"There's a restaurant a few blocks down with some outside seating. We need to request a certain table and some set things to eat and then wait."

I lifted my eyebrows, wanting to tell him that was a silly way of trying to get a message to someone. But I wasn't about to argue. I knew this information had come from Anthony's journal, and we didn't have anything else to go on. If I had to sit on a chair for a while and pretend to be interested in food, I could cope.

We walked to the restaurant together as if we were a couple on a date, talking about nothing much and trying to make it work between us. The thought amused me, given how I knew he'd felt about Anthony. I wasn't his type, and I was totally good with that.

Not sure what else to do, I let him take the lead once we got to the restaurant. It looked more upmarket than I was expecting, and I paused by the door, but Ben took my hand in his, really selling the couple act.

The host came up to us, picking up two menus as he did.

"I really need a seat at a table near the back. Not too much light, but enough we can see to stare into each other's eyes. And we'll have some water right away." Ben said, trying to sound confident in what he was asking for.

It took all my self-control not to laugh at the awkwardness of it and the way the host looked between us. It couldn't be easy, being on the receiving end of a strange request like that, but he nodded and led us deeper into the restaurant with purpose.

The tables were mostly full, but there was one booth down the side that was free that he led us to. The host handed us menus and hurried away to get the pitcher of water Ben had demanded already.

"We're ready to order," Ben said when the host reappeared and put the water down.

The man looked a little put out, but he beckoned over a waitress before hurrying off again.

"What can I get the two of you? We've got some specials, and I see you've got menus, but it sounds like you've already decided what you want."

"Yeah, we want the sharing platter for the starter, with extra garlic on the mushrooms. And then we want the carbonara with extra cheese and extra bacon, and some fries. Can we also get a dipping pot of the hot chocolate syrup? For the fries. It's better than ketchup."

When Ben made the order, she looked back and forth between us. Ben took my hand and grinned.

"I'll get right on it," she replied, as if we hadn't just made the weirdest order known to man. It made me chuckle.

"Fries and hot chocolate syrup?" I asked when we were alone.

"Yeah. Anthony said it was surprisingly yummy. Like sweet and sour or maple syrup on bacon. Some combinations work better than you'd think."

I shrugged, willing to try it when it arrived.

It was strange sitting there, knowing we were waiting for both a person and food. Or something to happen along with the food. We got through the starter together, however, and I was grateful we at least got that much. It was amazing and yummy and made a change from the limited menu I'd had to get used to while in the dragon city.

Because so many dragons had been funny about my color, I'd quickly learned there was only one place I could really eat and not be bothered, especially if my two protectors weren't around.

Going back to being just a regular human in a regular world held its appeal, as I devoured yet another garlic mushroom and followed it with a stringy warm mozzarella stick.

"Have you not eaten at all today?" Ben asked as I devoured another one.

"Sorry," I replied, slowing and waiting for him to eat some more.

"No. It's okay. I'm not a fan of this sort of food." He pushed the platter over to me and sat back.

Not about to argue, I finished it off, and then we were back to waiting.

We were halfway through the second course—we had both tried the fries in syrup combination and then proceeded to go back to eating the carbonara instead. I let Ben eat more of the main, eating some fries to supplement what I'd eaten.

Before we'd finished, a woman walked up and slid into the seat beside me.

"Fancy meeting you both here. I must admit I love the food here too."

"Here," I offered. "Try the fries in chocolate syrup. It's... yummier than you'd think."

She lifted her eyebrows as if I'd said the wrong thing and looked between the two of us.

"We've always loved the food here and come every month." Ben shot me a glare as he spoke. I shrugged. Ben hadn't mentioned anything about there being some kind of pass phrase, but I guess I'd just put my foot in it.

She seemed puzzled at first by the two of us but fixed her eyes on Ben. "Okay, well, this is a little unexpected. You do realize this is meant to be a place where we summon you, and not the other way around, right?"

"I know it's unconventional, but we've got some questions for you, if you'd be kind enough to answer them. A friend of ours who has met you here on more than one occasion is dead. And we want to get some answers as to why. He's left me and the girl here enough information deliberately to lead us to you."

"Deliberately? Our members aren't meant to give our information to anyone."

"We meant a lot to him. And his death was…not natural." I tried to look like it was a throwaway statement, but I'd basically told her that her usual contact had been killed.

"So the pair of you are investigating it?" The woman only frowned more at the explanation we were giving her.

"We think he's leading us to something he knew or understood about our kind. Something important no matter where our allegiances lie," Ben said, shooting me another look.

It was the shut-up look. I knew that, but I was tired of waiting and not understanding everything. "What are you hiding? Are you really working for an organization that is basically a terrorist cell, or are you trying to find another way to be heard and seen? We've been tangling with shadow catchers, and they killed Anthony. I want to know why and what he thought he was doing."

"Shadow catchers? Multiple of them?"

"Four."

She let out a low whistle and seemed to deflate.

"So far, it looks like the more of those things there are, the more important the target is. Is that right? Can either of you just confirm something like that for me?"

"We believe it is so," the woman replied, turning her body slightly so she could get a better view of me. "You strike me as a red dragon."

"How would you know?" I asked, feeling extra irritated.

"You're blunt and don't take prisoners. I can respect the fire inside you and how well it gets everything done. But know that a lot of others will inherently not trust it."

"I'm not asking you to trust me. Just tell me what you know about what could have caused my friend's death. He came to you, and after his death he's led us to you."

"Anthony was helping us look for the dragon holding the gate shut. It needs reinforcing, and we can't do it without the main alpha." She didn't miss a beat or look away from me.

"What do you mean?" Ben sat forward.

"The stories are all true. Please don't tell me that you believe the crap the dragon city elders spit out about the gate being completely fine and nothing being needed to keep it going. It needs a regular sort of top-up if nothing else." She paused to dip a french fry into the sauce. "The demon on the other side is actively trying to get out. If the gate is left alone and never given any extra power, eventually, the demon will work its way to the surface. And with each passing week, it grows stronger, and its minions and its shadow catchers get stronger along with it."

"Minions?" I asked, knowing I was interrupting but wanting more information.

"Yes. Now I can't say any more here. I didn't realize you were looking for something of your own, and I have to go looking for answers of another kind myself. If you're willing to come with me, I can possibly explain more, but you've got a few minutes, and that's all I can spare."

She slid back out of the booth, and I followed without hesitation. Before Ben could pay, our visitor did, the card bearing the name of "Jace." Our waitress put down a tray of drinks and hurried over to help us.

Jace strode to the door. I rushed after, determined to find out what was going on and appear confident.

Once I was outside, the light made me blink for a moment, and I almost lost sight of her as she moved away in the same purposeful manner. She went toward a nearby parking lot. Ben caught up to me and hurried along beside me. Instead of her getting into a car as I would have expected, she hurried from the parking lot and down between two restaurants.

"Okay, this is a little better and a shortcut to where I need to go."

"Thank you for taking the time to talk to us," I said, pretty sure it was the polite thing to say in the current situation.

"You don't sound like you know a damn thing about the enemy we should be facing together," she said as I fell in beside her. Not once did she look my way, but I gulped anyway.

"I've been in a sort of exile for a while. I don't know much about a lot of things I apparently ought to." I didn't like making the confession, but I had a feeling that being honest was going to get me further than anything else.

"The demon can turn a human or dragon into a sort of minion. It's not easy for him to do. And the host has to be willing to some degree. But it means they slowly get stronger as they are blessed with more of his power. And the shadow catchers answer to them. Some can control more shadow catchers, some only one or two. But they're all a problem, because they look like us."

I glanced at Ben, who had grown more serious. His forehead creased as his frown deepened. This wasn't good news for any of us.

"How do I know that you're telling me the truth?" Ben asked.

I gasped, but Jace did nothing more than glance his way.

"I've got no reason to lie to you about something that will make you suspect me or wish I was wrong. It's the truth. I'd say that you should ask the leaders of your city about it, but most of them lie these days. There's some who don't, but they're few and far between. And the rest are too young to remember anything different."

Ben opened his mouth to argue some more, but before he could, Jace stopped walking.

"Fuck," she said as I spotted what she had seen. There was a shadow catcher at the end of the alley, and it was coming our way. The creature was a hideous snake-like shadow with the legs of a centipede and a large beak on a bird-like head that came up from the body and swung back and forth. It wasn't the first time I'd seen one, but I shuddered in fear just the same.

As one, we all turned to try to get away from it.

"You two had better not be betraying me. The group won't take kindly to me not returning—"

"We're right along in here with you," I cut her off from getting shitty at us. "It would be a pretty stupid trap."

"It would." She stopped as another appeared at the other end, trapping us in place.

"What is it with these things appearing everywhere I go?" I said, growling the last word.

Ben looked around. "We need a way out."

"Our only option is up, but this is too narrow for a dragon morph." Jace looked up at the same time as I did anyway. Maybe we could climb.

There was nothing but bricks on either side of us, and I got the impression that none of us could manage that.

"What color dragon are you?" I asked as Jace reached behind herself and unhooked what looked like a small version of the shield the black dragons had used the last time we'd been running from shadow catchers.

"Black. Only way this works." She held up the very shield I was admiring.

"Then let me help. We're going to charge this shadow catcher together, but we need to all maintain contact for this to work," I replied.

Jace looked as if I'd grown three heads, but Ben placed a hand on her shoulder.

"Anthony believed in this dragon and asked me to bring

her to you. Please let us show you what she can do. Trust her and Anthony, even if you don't trust me."

Again, Jace hesitated, but there wasn't much else that could be done. The shadow catchers were in the alley with us, and we'd made enough noise that they knew exactly where we were.

"Okay. I'm putting my life in your hands, kid. You'd better know what you're doing after all."

I grinned and reached into the part of me that seemed to know what to do. Almost instantly, I felt the power flowing from all three of us and into the shield.

We ran as a group, charging faster and hanging onto each other until we hit the shadow catcher in front of us. It squealed in pain and was flung backward.

Our momentum carried us forward to the end of the alley and out into the open. None of us stopped running, however.

I continued, and Ben took my hand and pulled me away from Jace as she changed direction again.

A third shadow catcher appeared ahead of us, but a car pulled up and picked up our contact. Although I considered it, we were too far away to follow. She slammed the door behind her, taking her shield with her.

If Ben hadn't been tugging on my hand, there was no telling what I'd have done, but somehow he got me back to his car. I slipped into the passenger seat as he ran around the car and got us going.

For a second, I wasn't sure we could get around the three shadow catchers, even with one of them injured, but a large pickup truck came swinging into the parking lot and flashed on several bright lights, stunning the creatures momentarily and buying us time.

It was all the opportunity Ben needed to speed us away and down the road.

I exhaled, relief flooding through me and helping to calm my pounding heart. Somehow we'd survived yet another shadow catcher attack, learned a little bit more about Anthony, and Ben had vouched for me in front of a stranger.

Although I still had a lot of questions, it felt as if we'd at least achieved something.

CHAPTER SIX

When I woke in the morning, I found Ben sitting at my kitchen table with a mug of coffee. There were several rings around the inside of his mug at various levels, as if it had sat there for some time and been forgotten about, or he'd reheated it.

"Can't sleep?" I knew he hadn't been quite the same since our meeting with Jace the night before.

"No. I keep thinking about what she said. How he had been working for her. It's obvious from the journals that he is more comfortable with these people than I expected. But to work for them? It undermines everything the city stands for."

"Only if what you think about the city and about them as a group is true." I sat down and reached out a hand.

"It's what I've always believed to be true. But clearly, Anthony wasn't as bothered by it, or he didn't agree. Only nowhere in the journals so far has he explained any of it."

I looked into Ben's eyes. "Did you trust him?"

He nodded.

"Then keep trusting him and what he thought was best. He might not have been perfectly right, but whatever this is, Anthony thought it was important. He was putting time and effort into this group for some reason. It's up to us to find out why. Just like everything else, I'm sure he intends for us to work through it together."

"I'm not sure that I'm ready to find out that the city I believed in working for is lying to all its people."

"We don't know if that's true either. Maybe that was what Anthony was trying to work out. Maybe he was trying to keep me safe while he figured all this out too."

"Maybe… I wish he was here to ask. I wish I could talk to him about all the things he thought were best. About all his ideas and how he kept you safe for so long, but somehow I can't keep you safe inside the city or out for even five minutes. Other dragons and shadow catchers are almost always chasing you."

"I think something changed. They've only been chasing me as long as they were also after Anthony." I got up again and started to fix us both some breakfast, pretty sure that Ben must have been up all night worrying.

It wasn't easy to cope with the death of a loved one. I'd seen others fall apart, and some of the kids in the care homes with me had lost their parents when they were old enough to know about it. It wasn't pretty. But to have the danger on top, and the possible conspiracy theories, and a life that was under pressure from being hidden…

Everything was stacked against Ben being okay.

While we ate, we talked about the shadow catchers, minions, and what it all meant for us.

"Could someone else in the restaurant have called the shadow catchers to us?" I asked once we'd finished eating and I was ready to start thinking about it again.

"It's possible that there was a handler in the restaurant too."

"Handler? Is that what you call a minion?"

"Yes. It's what they're called in the city. Because they're meant to be humans, elves, and other mythical races who turned to demon worship by choice and now serve the great demon by choice so they could have more power and control his minions for him. Jace implied that there was a lot more to that problem than meets the eye. That some are sort of...enslaved to it."

"The truth might lie somewhere in the middle," I offered. "It often does with these things. No one story is right, but bring them all together and there's a chance that someone is on the right path and everyone is sort of right about some element of it."

"I think I remember Anthony saying something similar." Ben's eyes suddenly lit up and he hurried through to the kitchen where he'd left his bag and the journal. I had one of the spare journals, and the other was safe in the small apartment Ben had in the dragon city.

We both knew why he'd rushed. He'd thought of another phrase, and that meant that we had another shot at getting some more pages translated. That was something worth getting excited about. Not only had it been lovely to have a memento of Anthony, but it was taking us on a journey of self-discovery, it seemed.

With another set of pages translated and some more

guidance on what to expect from this shadowy organization, I felt a little better, but Ben wasn't convinced still.

"This gets more and more concerning. It reads as if the organization was already involved in something that Anthony was up to long before he tried to get information on you and keep you safe. They've known about you for a long time, and Anthony has known that there was something different about you."

"I'm not sure what that means." My blood ran cold anyway.

Whatever was happening, someone somewhere had asked Anthony to keep me safe, and we still had no idea who. And we only suspected that there was someone because of the journal. If that hadn't been explained, I'm not sure I'd have been comfortable with Anthony and Ben anymore.

After reading it all, my mind was made up. I was going to talk to this splinter group again. There were too many questions, and it was clear they had some of the answers. And Jace had seemed keen to tell me—she just hadn't wanted to defend me in battle with a shadow catcher. Or do anything to get herself into more trouble.

It wasn't an idea I expected Ben to be okay with, but as soon as I told him, he nodded.

"It's about the only path forward that might give us some idea of why all this is happening." Ben didn't look entirely happy, though.

"It bothers you?" I asked.

"A little, but it is just information. Just a meeting. And as long as we try to keep avoiding shadow catchers, then it is better than nothing. It feels wrong to have left the city for no good reason, and we're not expected back yet."

I nodded and got up. It left one thing to do. Go back to the restaurant and make the same strange order. Hopefully it would prove to be fruitful for a second time, and not a waste of our time.

Although it was earlier in the day, the same waiter was already working and lifted his eyebrow when he saw us and recognized us.

"Same seat as last time, please. And the same order."

The man nodded, clearly understanding that what we were really saying was that we wanted to talk to this strange dragon organization and Jace again.

"Come this way and I'll see how quickly we can sort you out."

I grinned, knowing he could be talking about both the food and the contact we wanted to meet.

This time I sat on the opposite side of the booth, wanting to be able to see a different angle of the restaurant and wondering if Jace would still choose to sit next to me or if she had a favorite seat. It was an odd thing to be curious about, but it just made me wonder.

We'd barely even finished the starter when a man strode into the fairly quiet establishment, bypassed all the staff, and came straight for our table. He sat himself down next to Ben, his mouth set in a thin line.

He was a well-built man, more broad shouldered than Ben, with a short haircut and simple slacks and shirt on, and for a moment I felt intimidated.

"You two had better have a good reason for calling on

us twice," he said, his gaze darting back and forth between Ben and me as if he expected one of us to explain.

"We got interrupted by shadow catchers last time," I replied, trying not to sound as if it was his fault.

"I'm aware. I was driving the car that picked up Jace yesterday. You cost her the task she had last night."

"I cost her?" I asked, feeling angry. This guy's tone and manner were full of contempt and annoyance. "The shadow catchers don't work for me. They're hunting something."

"Well, we don't want any more trouble from them or to bring us to their attention. None of us appreciates you being here again."

"Is that why you're here and not Jace?"

"I'm here because Jace isn't on duty and I am."

"And I am here because my mentor, Anthony, tasked me with interpreting his journal entries after he died. I don't know why. Not for sure. But I do know that he seemed to think you'd help me."

"Yes. I did promise to help his ward when the time came. Something about you being important and how you wouldn't have anyone in the world, and yet you show up with one of the city lot."

"To be fair to her, Anthony chose me for that too," Ben replied before I could say anything else.

This made the guy raise his eyebrows and look between us again.

"All right," he said after a pause. "What do you need help with?"

"What was it Anthony used to do for you?" I asked.

"He helped to gather information we needed, and in

return we passed him information now and then. And we helped him gather some tech he said he needed to survive."

"Tech?"

"Yeah. Some fancy stuff that was meant to be able to track the latent power of certain dragons and help funnel it into something more focused. I don't know if it ever worked, but it was fun watching him try."

I exhaled, trying to compute what I'd just heard.

"Now, how do I know that you're on the straight and narrow?" our contact asked. "Why can I trust you with anything?"

My mouth opened and shut a few times as I struggled to comprehend everything he had said and tried to think of the best way to explain.

I realized I had nothing. "In truth, you don't know you can trust us. Just as we don't know that we can trust you. But I have so many questions, and I think you have the answers."

"Wanting information is all well and good, but I think we all know that we're at a stage in the world and in our culture where information is the most valuable thing that any of us have. If you want to know something, then we need to exchange information, not have me give it to you for free."

Ben's hands bunched into fists, and I was pretty sure he'd have hit the person in front of us if he'd had the chance.

Instead I asked a question.

"What information was Anthony looking for, for you?"

"Anthony wasn't just looking for information. He was helping us. He wanted to find the same thing we did."

"And what's that?"

"The red dragon heir."

I exhaled, knowing what Anthony had implied with everything about me so far. He had appeared to be thinking I might be the heir.

"And you know who that is?" I asked, hoping the answer was yes and it wasn't me.

"No. And I wouldn't tell you even if the answer is yes. They need to be loved and nurtured. Whoever the heir is, they're young and not really ready for what they might have to do. Whoever finds them needs to show care."

"What are they going to have to do?"

"A lot of things, but at least unite all the dragons left alive in this world."

"All of them?" I asked, wondering how many there were and why this sounded like an insanely difficult task.

"What are they teaching about the gate in that city?" The guy lifted his eyebrows and studied me.

"You know the answer to that question. They're teaching that the gate is secure and it just requires us to remain alive and vigilant." Ben's eyes narrowed as he spoke, and I heard the annoyance in his voice. Ben definitely didn't like this guy.

"I need to know what Anthony wanted to know and why he was working with you all." I tried to bring the focus back on me.

"And if I trusted you the way we trusted him and you'd earned it like he did, then maybe that would be an okay request. But right now, it seems like you're asking an awful lot and not offering much."

I frowned. That wasn't the answer I'd hoped for. Both

Jace and he had seemed like they were willing to answer a lot of questions about everything. Even if Ben didn't agree with everything they were saying, they had been talking, and that was half the battle. Now, however... It was as if something had clammed him up.

"How could I earn your trust? I don't want to take sides or get in the way of anything you're doing, especially if you're genuinely trying to protect this planet from a demon. But I do need answers."

"Work for us. Prove you're willing to help us and don't have a problem with who we are, and give us your time and energy. It will free up one of our other people to have the time to get you the answers you seek. That's how our entire group works. Collective sharing of information. If you want some, you need to provide some."

"We're not—" Ben started to object until I lifted my hand.

He glared at me and reached out for me to leave with him as he got up. Shaking his head, he didn't take his eyes off me, but I still didn't get up to go with him.

"In all likelihood, I'll say yes to your offer, but it is something I want to think about first. I don't think I should rush into an agreement with you, no matter how much I want to know about Anthony. If I give you an answer, I want to be sure I can follow through."

"That's wise of you, I must admit, and for that, you have my respect. If you do want to work with us, just come back here anytime this week and leave a postcard of the Hollywood sign. We'll then meet you there that night at midnight."

"Got it. Thank you for coming to meet me today."

The guy got up and gave me and Ben a nod before hurrying away. Only a few seconds later, the waitress arrived with our main course. Shrugging, Ben sat back down, and we tucked in. There was no point in us not eating it now. We were going to have to pay for it, and we had nowhere else to be.

CHAPTER SEVEN

For the first few minutes, Ben and I ate in silence, and I felt the tension between us. I felt worried too, but I couldn't see a better course of action. There were so many unknowns, and I wanted answers.

We ate the carbonara and fries quickly, beginning to talk about little nothings before we were done, the way we usually did when we shared a meal. The normal behavior helped calm me.

"You really want to do this, then?" he asked after we'd paid and were back in the car. Despite us being ready to go, he didn't pull out or do anything but start the engine.

"I don't see what other option we have." I turned in my seat to face him, trying to work out how angry he was, but he only stared ahead with his hands on the steering wheel, as if he were driving.

"There are plenty of other options. The city elders are sure that we're safe. Yes, we've lost our line of rulers, and yes, there are things we don't understand about the gate and how it holds the demon at bay, but it does and it has for millennia. To some degree, we just have to trust that."

"But what if these people are right? What if there is more to it? What if they are doing something important?"

"Then there are better ways to go about it. It's not as simple as just finding a red dragon heir and putting them in charge."

I paused, feeling the anger in Ben and not entirely sure where it was coming from. It didn't make much sense. And I wasn't sure I wanted to argue with him. Even if they were wrong, Anthony had seen something in what they were doing, and I felt as if I had to take the chance that it meant something. I had to believe that he had a reason for all this and was genuinely doing what was best for me.

Slowly, Ben calmed down, and I waited for him to say something again. I wasn't sure what else to do. We needed to be in agreement. So far, everything we'd done to find out what Anthony had been up to, we had done together. I didn't want to start doing something without Ben now.

"There needs to be some kind of plan for us moving forward," Ben said eventually, clearly an awful lot calmer.

"I agree. And I think it's better if we can find a course of action we agree on together. Anthony always wanted us to do this together. There's a lot I still don't know. A lot that I might be wrong about, and there's also possibly things that the elders are wrong about. I think we need to keep an open mind, but I don't want to force or push you to do something that really isn't comfortable for you either."

"It's not that I'm not comfortable. I don't think I'll ever be happy with the idea of working with a group of dragons who are known for being terrorists in one form or another. But I think you're right. Anthony saw something in what they were doing, and I don't think either of us will be able to sleep at night if we don't try to find out what."

"Thank you," I replied a few seconds later.

"I just hope this leads to some kind of next part of the code. With any luck, Anthony can tell us himself what it was he intended and we can stop trying to guess and figure it out."

"Sounds like a—"

A knock on the car window made me jump. I didn't finish my sentence as I instead looked at the man standing on the other side. Ben pressed the button on the side of his steering wheel to lower the window.

"Forgive me for interrupting your conversation, but I saw you a little while ago in the restaurant and I think I may have picked up on you two being...more than meets the eye. Is that true?"

"That would depend on why you're asking," Ben replied while I stared at the older man.

He walked with a cane and had a shocking mass of unruly white hair on his head. I wasn't sure what to say and didn't entirely feel comfortable so close to a stranger after all the trouble we'd been having and the mysterious way he was approaching us.

"I am like you. Not affiliated with any particular city, although I was once near Washington. Many times I've seen someone you may know, one of our kind called Anthony. I've even seen him once or twice with young Scarlet here, although it took me a moment to place you."

My mouth fell open. How did this guy know me?

Ben got out of the car and came around to my side.

"What do you know of Anthony?" Ben asked as the guy backed up.

Worried that something bad was going to happen and able to hear the anger and fear in Ben's voice, I got out and tried to work out what had got Ben so riled up. Surely there was no harm in a guy knowing Anthony?

"I don't know a lot. Just that I respected him and he clearly cared for Scarlet here. A few times I sort of worked with him. Helped him get information he needed. He was looking into the red bloodline. And with a friend called Scarlet around, it doesn't take a genius to work out why." The older guy held his hands up in a defensive, please-believe-me pose.

Although this seemed to satisfy Ben enough that he stopped bristling and tried to appear casual, there was still tension in the air.

"What was he looking into, exactly?" I asked, deliberately keeping my voice softer and trying to get everyone focused on a single problem at a time.

"I'm afraid I don't know the exact questions he was asking… My specialties are more related to getting out of places again after acquiring what you need. If you need someone to help you plan an escape, or items and apparel in case of an emergency encounter with something unpleasant, I can make it easier for people who are in need of being discreet to appear to blend in."

"So you're an escape artist with a side in master of disguise." I didn't expect much of a response, but I gained a slight laugh out of it. It made me feel like I hadn't said something completely foolish.

"Something like that, my child. Anyway, I wanted to

offer you my support in your endeavors. I can be found in many places, but this method never fails to reach me." As he finished speaking, he pulled out a small business card.

Instead of handing it to Ben, he gave it to me. I was about to tuck it away when there was a shout from nearby.

All three of us walked closer to investigate. We had to go around the side of the restaurant as more people shouted and a woman yelped. We heard the sound of screeching metal a moment later.

It felt strange to be heading toward what sounded like danger, but there was something about being part of a group of dragons that made me braver, especially knowing that I could combine the powers of several of us to at least stun a shadow catcher. Of course, not all danger was related to us and the strange creatures that appeared to be hunting me.

"Now look what's happened," a guy yelled, his torso covered in a tight t-shirt that showed off the muscular contours underneath. "You've only gone and bent the front fender."

I exhaled when I saw the shouting was about something entirely human and normal. No evil lurking in the shadows. Ben visibly relaxed, his shoulders lowering and his fists unbunching.

The three of us watched as a woman backed up the car that had been damaged and others came over to help. Not wanting to get involved in something that wasn't really any of our business, I turned to walk back to our car.

Despite the early hour, I felt tired. It had already been emotional, and I was ready to sleep or chill out somewhere. But there was still a very interesting man beside me, and when he'd mentioned that he knew Anthony, a part of me wanted to ask him to stay and tell me everything.

Because we didn't know exactly what Anthony had been up to, I felt that it wasn't important to rush through anything where we didn't have to, and this felt like one of those situations.

"It has been a pleasure to meet you, Scarlet, and you…" The newcomer trailed off as he held out his hand to shake Ben's.

My new mentor hesitated before taking the offered hand and shaking it. I thought they might end up having some kind of disagreement, but it passed. I noticed that Ben didn't offer his name, however.

I was still reeling from processing all the new information and all these people. It was strange to think that I'd met so many dragons outside of the dragon city when the majority of our kind were meant to be keeping out of the spotlight.

The old guy shuffled away and leaned on his cane. Worried that my lack of response was stopping him from leaving when he looked weary, I reached for the card he had given me.

"Thank you, Fintar," I said, reading the name on the business card. "I hope we see you around soon."

A few more muffled grunts and yells from behind the restaurant drew our attention again.

"What the hell is that?" the same guy yelled.

This time, my blood ran cold. I didn't need to go check to know I was hearing the panic of several people seeing a shadow catcher, or something equally as vile.

Fearing the worst, I wasn't sure whether I should run toward it or away from it. I wasn't used to running away from danger, but equally, I wasn't convinced that I would be capable of facing it head on. Not when there had been so many close calls and there was already so much fear around me.

But Ben went back to check and Fintar went with him. No matter what I thought wise, I definitely wasn't going to be left alone.

Everyone was pointing at something as we got closer, and there were too many human bodies in the way for me to be sure what they were all looking at. For several seconds we didn't move. I could only hope it wasn't a shadow catcher.

"What's it doing?" someone else asked.

"It's like it's sniffing the air. Or listening."

"Listening," I said under my breath, able to imagine one of them and what they were most likely to be doing right now. Although they could smell, they seemed to navigate more by hearing than scent.

And it doing both together was scary. From where it was, however, it couldn't smell me. I wasn't close enough. But I could be heard.

Slowly, I backed up, reaching out for Ben's arm to encourage him to follow me. It was almost reflexive, and he leaned toward me though he didn't actually move his feet.

I turned, wanting to get back to the safety of the car, but another scream came from that direction.

There was another shadow catcher near our car, and it was heading closer in broad daylight.

"Ben," I called, throwing caution to the wind as I stared at the creature getting closer to the car. So much of our stuff was in that car, including the first and main copy of Anthony's journal. It wasn't something we could just leave and walk away from.

"Hurry," he said, instantly understanding what I was worried about.

Together, we ran for the car, and I tried to figure out if there was anything we could do to put the current shadow catcher off its goal of heading to our belongings. It seemed intent on going for it and not toward us, which was unlike them so far.

I didn't hesitate, however, yelling and trying to get its attention for a while so Ben could run around and get to our stuff first.

For a moment it didn't look as if it was going to work at all, but eventually the shadow catcher turned its beak-tipped snout in my direction and swayed in place.

Stopping, I regarded it while it appeared to study me. It was the normal sort of shadow catcher at first glance, but it held itself in a slightly different way, almost as if it had gained something as we'd got closer. Something I couldn't quantify.

I approached more warily, aware I would have to run suddenly, but it didn't move.

While I seemed to have some kind of standoff with the creature, Ben snuck around the side and toward our vehicle. Thankfully, the journals and notebooks we needed above all else were on the side of the car Ben could get to more easily.

As the shadow catcher's attention seemed to sway and

the noise of Ben approaching grew louder, I took another step nearer, wanting to keep it still and focused on pinpointing me.

Coughing, I got it to swing its head back toward me, but as Ben opened the car door, it appeared to make up its mind finally. It lunged at the old hunk of metal, and when it touched the car door, the whole thing seemed to rust before my eyes, then crumple and fall apart until there was nothing but a pile of scrap metal.

It kept going as Ben grabbed the bag with the journals and translations and yanked it out. He was just in time to stop everything from being reversed or decayed, or whatever it was the shadow demons did to everything they touched.

Ben hurried back around to me as the creature flailed in the car and destroyed our clothes and the leather upholstery. It seemed to be eating the engine and car parts as well.

"Come with me," Fintar said as Ben rejoined us. The shadow catcher finally seemed to understand that we were on the other side of the scrap heap he'd turned our car into.

I could almost feel the anger in the shadow catcher, but I ignored it and let Fintar wave the pair of us over and after him. It appeared as if we were going to get to find out exactly how good this guy was at impromptu escape plans.

We followed him across the parking lot, not even really trying to go around any of the traffic.

If we'd been more wealthy, and not needed every last possession we owned, and if the car hadn't had any sentimental attachments, it would have been totally fine.

But the car represented our freedom through the various journeys we'd been on. Now it was a heap of junk and we were going to have to find something else to take us back to the dragon city. It didn't seem fair to lose another of the things that mattered to us.

As the first shadow catcher came around the main building, I was pretty sure that we'd have a problem trying to outrun them. Without the use of a vehicle, we could only go so far.

"This way," Fintar added.

I didn't hesitate to follow. He was sure of a plan, and I was getting tired of running from these creatures. They were hounding me at every turn.

The guy ran to a car and unlocked it by reaching into his pocket and pressing a button on a remote entry key.

Although we were barely ahead of the shadow catchers, we had enough time to dive inside while our savior started the engine. He pulled forward and away from the nearest demon spawn a fraction of a second before it would have hit his car and destroyed it as well.

For a few more seconds I stayed where I was, sprawled on the back seat beside Ben, not sure I wanted to move or sit up or even put a seat belt on.

Ben was the first to move and get himself strapped in, and I reluctantly followed suit.

Over the next few minutes, I tried to process everything that was happening as Ben directed our savior to help us get to another car so we could sort ourselves out.

Within an hour, we were there and safe. It turned out Anthony had a spare car that Ben had known about as well.

I'd never seen him drive it, but it wasn't a surprise to either of the dragons I was with.

"When a dragon leaves the city for a good reason, we often have cars and other means of transport sorted in case of emergencies," Ben explained when I failed to hide my shock.

"It's important that we can always get back among our kind. But now that you are both safe, I must continue. It has been an honor to meet a red dragon at last, especially one such as yourself," Fintar said. "I hope we meet again soon."

He walked away, his cane tapping as he leaned on it, and then drove away. It was only as the car pulled out that I realized I had seen him run with us and not struggle at all, but now he appeared as if he was too weak to walk unaided.

Before I could point it out to Ben, however, he ushered me into the new car. I was immediately hit by how like Anthony it was. My chest ached with a longing to see him again. It felt as if no matter how much time passed, it was going to hurt.

CHAPTER EIGHT

Sitting on the sofa in my apartment made everything feel better again. So many times I had retreated here to feel better and stop worrying about everything. It was good to be back, even if it made me miss Anthony more.

A part of me felt as if this wasn't entirely home in the same way anymore. The dragon city had become part of my life as well. It had been difficult at points, but I wasn't the same person as I had been while I had been living here. And it felt strange sitting in the same place as the old me had.

"This is a difficult situation and make no mistake," Ben said as he sat down opposite me. "I don't know what to do. It's not a feeling I'm used to. Something is still drawing the shadow catchers to you. And there's all this talk of heirs and information and the demon and gates, and I don't know what's right or wrong anymore."

"Do we have to know what's right yet?" I asked.

Ben opened his mouth and then closed it and thought.

"I'm worried that the longer we don't know what's truly

going on, the longer you're in danger unnecessarily. You were safe in the dragon city."

"But we weren't getting any answers, and neither of us was getting closure on what Anthony died for. He believed something was worth his life."

"Very true, but it's also now my responsibility to make sure that you don't lose *your* life because we're not careful enough." Ben looked straight at me as he spoke, and the weight of this task seemed to squash down his shoulders.

I took both his hands in mine and didn't look away.

"I think we both know that I'm more capable of keeping myself safe than Anthony realized. That like other red dragons and the rumors of what they were capable of, I seem to be able to do more."

"You do seem to be…gifted…in ways that I hadn't expected."

"Then let us trust what's happening so far. Trust what we do know we can do and keep going down this path. Anthony seemed to think this was needed to some degree. And he trusted you. I trust you."

Ben squeezed my hands and nodded. We had a sort of agreement.

"I know you have misgivings, but I think we should work with this splinter group Anthony trusted. They want to help us figure out what he was looking into, and we can see what they're asking of us."

"Given the only other option is to go back to the city and give up, I think you're right. I must warn you that we need to be careful. If the elders in the city realize what we are doing, there could be…issues."

I sat back and thought about this warning. While I

didn't like being told what I could and couldn't do, life wasn't black and white. If the elders of the city had a problem with this organization and Anthony had been hiding his affiliation, then I was sure that we were going to be walking into something not entirely right.

Not doing anything wasn't an option, however. I was being hunted. I needed to know why.

With that in mind, Ben left me in the apartment so he could deliver the postcard and get some food for us while we waited for midnight and our chance to meet up with our contact again. It felt very strange to be sitting around and doing nothing much after the last few weeks of constant lessons, learning, and trying to adjust—or run from creepy monsters.

Somehow, I managed to fill the time with a book until Ben returned with food. We ate and I showed him the favorite board game I played with Anthony in the past.

The time ticked by and I started to relax a little. At least, until it got closer to midnight and we had to go back out again. Not only were we meeting someone from the splinter group, but it would put us in danger once more. It also meant our short reprieve was over.

I went from calm to antsy and fidgety so quick, Ben eventually rolled his eyes and grabbed my jacket.

"Come on. Let's get out there to see if it calms you down at all," he said as he handed it to me.

There was no way I was going to argue with him, so we got back in the strange new car and made our way to the Hollywood sign. Even this late at night, it was fairly busy and we weren't the only ones there.

It seemed as if we would miss our contact or they

would miss us, but just being up there made me feel better. I could see the city below and the lights and cars moving around it. It was beautiful but also haunting in its relative safety—so many people, and none of them worried about whether they would survive a night or not.

Most of them went about their lives and worried about smaller things like bills and who loved them or not, and what they were going to do at special events or wear to parties. They didn't have to worry about creatures that chased them, if the other dragons in their city were going to wear them down so much they made a deadly mistake, or if they were heir to the throne of an entire species and possibly responsible for keeping an entire world safe.

I tried to push the last thoughts from my head. There was no sense dwelling on something like that. I wasn't going to be saving anything if I couldn't figure out what was going on.

We continued to mill around, walking slow circles around the letters and trying not to get in anyone else's way until it was several minutes after midnight. Despite the fact that the night was warmer than some lately, I was getting cold and considered giving up.

This was all so crazy. My life had become insane.

"This way," Jace said, appearing to our left, and not looking pleased to be there. She barely looked at us as she walked away from the sign.

I almost asked her where she thought we were going to go, but I was so eager to get on with it that I followed her anyway. It was strange that she felt she needed to take us somewhere else when we'd already met her here.

"Given the propensity for shadow catchers to turn up

wherever you do with no decent explanation, you'll have to forgive me for being extra careful," she said as she walked us toward a clearing in the nearby trees, where another strange sight met us.

A very large and very full wading pool sat there, although I had no idea how it had been filled. It went a long way to explaining why she had been late to meet us. Wasting no time, she emptied her pockets and stuffed everything in her shoulder purse, then got into the pool and waded to the middle. I pulled my phone from my pocket and followed. I wanted the safety net too.

For a second, I thought Ben wasn't going to join us at all, but eventually he climbed in, sloshing the cold water around and gasping at it.

"Can't you just make it warm?" I asked when he shivered alongside me. It only came up to just above our waists, but it was enough that we'd be safe from shadow catchers.

He looked so shocked that he'd forgotten his own power that it was almost as if I'd slapped him. A moment later, the water grew warmer and all of us felt better.

"Okay, I understand that you might want to take my partner up on an offer to work with us in exchange for something," Jace began.

"Yes," I replied. "I want to know what Anthony was looking for and what he knew, especially about red dragons and the demon gate."

"That's something he'd already been searching for, and for a long time. I can't promise that we'll be able to give you exactly what you need. But we were helping him as best we could."

"I just want to find out why Anthony has been leading me this way and what those creepy creatures want. What do you need me to do?"

I thought she was going to say no, but after a few seconds she smiled.

"There's not actually anything I can ask you to do right now, but knowing that you're eager helps. We don't want to force anyone to do anything."

I frowned, surprised by this turn of events. Her being keen to get me on board and then not actually give me anything to do was not the result I'd expected.

She tilted her head to the side and studied me.

"What did you say that your name was?"

"I didn't," I replied. "You implied that Anthony had mentioned me."

"That is true. Forgive me. For a moment I wondered if I was missing something, but I know Anthony was a good dragon. If he was taking care of you, then I trust this. It will take time for everyone else in our cell to feel the same, but I'm sure that they'll come around."

"Thanks, I think."

"And what of me?" Ben asked. "She's now my ward. Anthony entrusted me to continue looking out for her after his death."

"Is this true?" Jace asked me, looking between the two of us.

"Entirely. Ben has been looking out for me for several weeks now."

"Okay, then as long as you're both working together, we'll treat you as one team that Anthony vouched for. We'll contact one or other of you on this." Jace stopped speaking to pull out a small phone from her purse and handed it over.

"Keep it charged and don't use it for anything else. Don't let anyone know you have it, and follow any instructions that come through to it. If you have any questions, send them to the only number stored in contacts."

I took it before Ben could, feeling as if this might be a bit overkill for a way to contact each other. Did things really need to be this secret? But I knew the answer to this question, at least partially.

Anthony had been so careful, and I needed to be as well. And on top of that, I'd learned that red dragons were rare, some people wanted to find an heir, and some people thought we were egotistical, power-hungry maniacs. In short, few liked us, and if they did, they wanted us to rule and keep them safe.

I was starting to understand why some red dragons went off the rails and did things that others didn't like. They felt used or abused. Everyone had an opinion and no one seemed to be sure of the exact truth when it came to the reds. It made it even more important to me that I found the truth in as unbiased a way as possible. But how did I do that?

Before I could ask Jace any other questions, or what to expect from our first mission, another dragon in human form came rushing up.

"Shadow catchers coming this way. Two of them. They're following her trail." The guy pointed at me, his gaze full of accusation.

I folded my arms across my chest and moved farther

into the large wading pool. Jace did the opposite, however, and hurried to the edge to get out.

Ben grabbed my shoulder and pulled me away.

"Time to go," he whispered. "We're not going to learn any more today."

I wanted to argue and demand answers, but he was right. Once more, my color had prejudiced a bunch of dragons against me and I was going to have to prove I wasn't like the other red dragons. And all while being a red dragon and proud of it. To be me, but not in a negative way.

We retreated as the shadow catchers appeared on the other side of the clearing, and pulled back into the shadows. For a short time we didn't draw attention to ourselves and made sure we moved into the woodland quietly. It wasn't something we could keep up, however, and I soon made the faintest useful light I could with my finger. One of the other good things about my recent lessons was being able to control my ability better. I could now use a much smaller body part and make a much fainter light than before.

Ben helped guide us both back by going in a wide curve around the clearing, and then we picked up speed as we rejoined the path back to the Hollywood sign.

By the time we were back in the car I was exhausted. I almost cried frustrated, tired tears as Ben pulled away and left the shadow catchers and all the danger behind again.

While it felt as if being in a car with Ben was one of the few times that I was safe in this world, it was also a lot like running away. But we had nowhere to go now but back to the dragon city.

And we'd achieved hardly anything on this trip.

"It will get easier," Ben assured me after a few minutes. "Once the dragons in the city realize that you're not a threat, and if we can prove that Anthony knew something important, it should get easier."

I sighed and tried to calm down and dry my tears. Ben was supporting me as best he could, even with our disagreements. I wasn't alone, and that meant it could be worse.

As I calmed, I explained my thoughts in the pool. How I was starting to understand the other dragons' reactions and my fears about becoming like other red dragons.

"I don't think you're like the others. And neither did Anthony."

"But he was willing to assume I might be royalty."

"Given what we've told you of your color, that's actually a fairly logical assumption. You're possibly descended from a royal line in some way. But that doesn't mean you are for sure. Anthony definitely thought you were important either way."

"Which means that it will be easy for me to fall into the same attitude and behavior. I could develop a huge ego or become rebellious."

"You're already pretty rebellious," Ben replied without missing a beat. He grinned and I wasn't sure whether to be amused or irritated.

"I'm pretty sure I've been taught to be rebellious by Anthony. He did up and leave the dragon city."

"Nah, he did that because my feet smell." The smile on his face grew even wider. "Couldn't stand it. You have cute, dainty feet that always smell fresh."

"Are you saying he had a foot fetish?" I asked, doing everything I could to sound serious.

Ben's eyes went wide and he looked as if he'd made a horrific mistake.

I burst out laughing and soon Ben was chuckling too.

Silence fell as we grew more serious again, the tense atmosphere going with it.

"If it eases your mind, I will help you navigate who you are and what that means, and help you learn to handle whatever it turns out you are," Ben said a few minutes later. "I'll help *you* become *you* despite any legacy your color has."

"Thank you," I replied, grateful it was dark and he wouldn't be able to see the tears forming in my eyes. I might not know who I was, but I had a friend who planned to help me find out.

CHAPTER NINE

Groaning, I tried to stay asleep a little while longer, but I heard Ben moving and it wasn't long before I heard the sound of another voice. Flick was here.

I leaped out of bed, embarrassment at being caught in bed enough to make me blush and adrenaline to flood through me. Getting dressed in record time, I thought through the explanation I was meant to give my two self-appointed bodyguards around the city about where I'd been.

Within ten minutes I was walking from the bedroom and smiling at Flick as if I had no idea he was there. It would have been more effective if Ben hadn't smiled and winked and made it clear that he knew I had only just gotten up. It made me wonder if Ben had summoned Flick to get me out of bed.

This was officially Ben's apartment and, while I was his ward, I was considered old enough to have my own small room in the same tower. It was only because we felt I'd be safer with him that I wasn't sleeping there. But it did mean I was taking Ben's bed every night.

"Ready to go get some breakfast?" Flick asked.

There was no way I was going to argue with the thought of breakfast. I almost never ate with Ben, partially because I didn't want to invade his life entirely, but also because he wasn't the best cook, though he insisted on trying.

We'd not gone very far before Neritas joined us as well and I sat with Neritas at a table out of the way while Flick fetched a giant stack of pancakes and as much maple syrup as he could carry.

Although I often drew stares and looks when out in the public areas, they were no doubt noticing that I had been served far more food than usual. The chef must have picked up on my absence and decided to feed me up.

The pancakes tasted amazing after a couple of days of having to eat whatever there was, and then the strange meals at the restaurant two days in a row. I hadn't done a good job of taking care of myself, either. When you're running from demon creatures and trying not to cry a lot, food is often far from your mind.

"So, spill the beans. What did you head out of the city for?" Neritas asked as soon as we'd begun tucking into the pancakes and the restaurant had emptied out a little.

"It's...complicated," I replied at first, my rehearsed explanation vanishing from my head as soon as he asked.

"Of course it's complicated." Flick shook his head. "You're the first red dragon in the city in several years, the dragon who'd been watching you is dead, Ben is acting funny, and you are taking all this in your stride as if you expected it."

"I definitely didn't expect it." I shifted uncomfortably on my seat and tried to focus on the pancakes.

"Maybe not. But it's crazy. So why did the elders let you leave the city?" Flick asked and Neritas stared at me. One of them might be speaking, but both of them wanted answers.

I exhaled and tried to think of what I'd agreed with Ben. Some of it came back to me. As I looked at the two dragons who had spent the last three weeks by my side whenever I wasn't in Ben's apartment, I felt as if I owed them more. They had been protecting me too, even if they didn't have the reason Ben did.

"I'm not sure I can tell you both everything, but I'll be as honest as I can." I thought through my possible alternatives. "I've been left some instructions from Anthony. He wants me to complete something he was doing. It's likely related to me or the red dragons."

"*Something?*"

"That's where it's complicated. He hasn't explained it very well."

"So, some dead dragon has got you solving some puzzle to figure out what he was doing and why he hasn't reported you. Ben is helping you because he cared about the dead one and now you're trying to be careful in case it's something really bad?" Flick sat back, processing.

"Something like that. Except I'm not sure what it is. Please keep it to yourselves. Not even the elders know. At least I don't think they do. Ben said that he didn't tell them anything other than I needed to go back to the city for personal reasons. I know that's not the first time he's said that, though, and I think they're getting irritated with it."

"Yeah. As a general rule, only those who have been vouched for or who have proved they would be able to handle it are allowed out of the city these days." Neritas spoke for the first time in a while to explain.

"Why?" I asked. "It's not that dangerous out there. Just a human society to live in, but it's not that different from here."

"I think they're scared. And can you blame them?" Neritas asked. "The world isn't how it used to be. It's harder and harder to go anywhere without bumping into humans, and the humans are so wasteful and antagonistic that they don't make it easy to hide our powers. And that's without even taking into account the recent shadow catcher activity."

"I can understand the fear to some degree. The only part that bothers me is how unwilling so many are to change. And how people and dragons try to do things because that's how they've always done it or for the sake of nostalgia, and it keeps people locked into patterns that aren't good for them."

"Anyone with a mind can see some of that is true, but if you study history, there's also a fair bit of people simply not learning from their mistakes and assuming everyone new is going to be out to get you until they prove otherwise." Neritas ate his last bite and sat back. I didn't appreciate being lectured, but I wasn't sure he truly meant his words so I decided to give him the benefit of the doubt.

There was silence after this statement while I finished my pancakes as well. It was strange to be talking to two guys about something I'd barely even told anyone, but they seemed to process the information well. Flick was broody about it, but he thawed a little when I gave him a hug and thanked him, even though there wasn't a lot to be thanking him for.

"What are you going to do now?" Neritas asked as he flicked a suspicious glance at Flick. It was hard not to be a little bit devilish and respond with "your mom" or "your face" to Neritas' question. I did my best to resist the urge and actually say something helpful.

"I'm not sure. I need to carry on going to classes while I'm here and getting some decent grades… There's…life, though, and it gets in the way of at least some of my plans."

"What are your plans? Maybe we can modify things together." He rubbed his hands in glee.

Not sure what I should say, I sat back and thought about it. I didn't know how much of this I should tell them either. They were trying to be sweet, but it wasn't that simple. They could just be acting that way. How well did I know them, really? And I was also worried about Ben and what he'd say to me even being this open.

"The plan is mostly to stay alive, love life as much as I can, obey the rules of the city, and try to not die." I caught Flick's gaze and realized that he didn't buy it either. What would it take to get these two to put their focus on something else? Anything else.

"That's…not what I expected you to say," Neritas replied, a frown flitting across his face and making me wonder what he thought of me. I hadn't always considered what a person might be feeling and thinking before. Now, however, I contemplated it, trying to gauge whether he was bothered or not.

"It will have to wait. It's time to get to our first class," Flick said as he got up.

Although a part of me wanted to stay and talk, I also got up and tried not to look back. There were classes to go to and a sort of plan to unfold. Somehow this needed to be enough to keep me going.

There weren't many lessons in a week that I didn't share with Neritas and Flick, but they were difficult for me to go to. Having the pair of them act like bodyguards was an added bonus. Of course, it was very rare to bring your own bodyguard to anything. From the stares I got, I guessed that no one else had ever been accompanied everywhere the way I was.

Feeling strangely overwhelmed, I went through the motions of going to class and letting Flick steer our trio. I'd probably lost a bunch of human friends and I was pretty sure it was going to get worse before it got better. I didn't want to lose these two friends or Ben when I'd only just begun to make them. I needed someone in my life.

On top of that, my classes didn't fill me with warm, happy thoughts. They would often drag out, and teachers tried to explain history and situations where I was missing context and information that the people who were born here innately knew. Lessons for those who actually had the mental energy left to concentrate and ask the right questions.

"Right, good day to all of you. Welcome back, Scarlet," my teacher said, drawing attention to the fact that I'd been gone. Those who hadn't already known pricked up their ears and paid attention. I could have hit something.

Instead, I focused on what I had to do. Normally I was okay in this class—it was just that I hadn't expected to be put on the spot.

It was a cooking class. Not that it was a problem to learn something so normal as cooking, but it left a little to be desired when it came between much more interesting lessons.

I'd been to school before, even if the dragon city didn't entirely recognize it. The teachers were making me do several recipes and trying to get me to trip up and make something bad to eat, but every recipe I chose, I got right. Flick and Neritas made happy noises while eating my food and rescued me from being grilled afterward. And that was satisfying.

One of the best things about being a girl in the system had been the old people who wanted to teach me random useful skills. And they liked to talk. Since I liked not being noticed and was happy to listen, I had picked up a thing or two about baking, cooking, and how to make dishes taste better with subtle differences.

Thankfully, no one tried to ruin what I was doing this time. It would have been hard to do so today—we were learning a simple, one-pot rice dish, and I could make sure it was never unattended. It helped that I had learned to get all the utensils and receptacles I needed before I began preparing anything, so I never had to go far from my workstation.

Because it was such a simple dish, we were sharing our stations and ovens with other dragons. My "partner" was a dragon I'd never worked with before, but I knew of her. Tiffany. Of all the other dragons, she was one of the better ones in the kitchen, but she was young.

"Hi," I said, not sure if she was going to be friendly or not.

She gave me a nod, almost as if she was too shy to say anything.

Grateful that she wasn't being nasty, I considered this an improvement and focused on my cooking. As I did, I noticed she had a similar approach to baking, and she had all her equipment already as well. She was a little behind me, however.

When I realized she had forgotten a garlic press, I finished using mine and handed it to her.

"Thanks," she said as she took it and finally met my gaze.

"I hate having to stop in the flow of a recipe to get something," I replied, wondering if she'd take the offered conversation topic.

"I do too. It knocks me out of what I'm doing and then I'm more likely to forget an ingredient. Or add one twice."

"And we definitely don't want twice the paprika in this dish." I grinned, enjoying the conversation and friendly back and forth. It felt like a breath of fresh air.

"Oh gosh, no. There's almost no way back from that one."

"I had to try once. Ended up just adding almost double everything else and taking home the extra. Not sure how I got away with it, but I did."

She looked at me with wide eyes and got back to her

cooking. A few seconds later she introduced herself and smiled again.

Sure that I might have made my first friend in about two weeks, I asked her about herself and if she liked cooking, then listened while we prepped and made our one-pot meals.

By the time we were done, it was almost the end of the lesson and we'd swapped a few stories about growing up and how we'd first learned to cook. Her great-aunt worked for one of the big city restaurants—that's how Tiffany had caught the cooking bug. I loved hearing about it, and I'd probably eaten something in the last three weeks that her great-aunt had cooked.

When we were taste tested and scored, we ended up being the top two in class, and we both got some dirty looks. Much to my dismay, Tiffany even got a boo or two for the first time. I'd had them many times before, but I was used to them and didn't have a place to work that required thick skin, like she did.

"Sorry that they gave you a hard time for talking to me." I tried to sound as casual as possible.

"It's okay. It's shown me that I can't just keep going and ignore the problems of the world. We all have to pick sides eventually."

Her words were wise and commendably mature for her age, and made me even more grateful for her companionship during the lesson. She seemed to genuinely want to be friends, so I vowed to do what I could to protect her from any response the others might give that was less than agreeable.

The age gap between us was bigger than I hoped, but also it gave her an innocence that I couldn't manufacture.

"See you next class and thanks for your help!" she called as she hurried off.

Unable to move freely in the throng, I was pushed along with the other kids until Flick spotted me again and everyone got out of his way.

"Make me something yummy?" he asked.

"Who says it's for you?"

"You always make too much and let me and Neritas have some."

I stopped moving immediately and just stared at him. He was right, but I hadn't realized it until he'd said it.

"Don't tell me that you're now regretting it."

"It depends what you think it means."

"You like cooking to calm your emotions and you have a bad sense of portion size. I'm totally lucking out. I've not eaten so well since I was living with my mom."

I burst out laughing and handed him the spare dish I'd already plated up for him. At least I wasn't flirting accidentally.

CHAPTER TEN

As Flick, Neritas, Tiffany and Ben all sat down to eat together, I tried not to let the nerves get to me. I'd cooked for all of them before and not been worried about it, but it had been just handing out what I'd made in class. This was different. I had deliberately made a meal for all of them.

Not that I'd entirely chosen to make the meal. This was part of the cooking class too, to prove that I knew what I was doing. Ben had suggested we feed everyone I knew and was friends with.

I think he'd expected, or hoped, that there would be more of us. If he had, he kept his disappointment to himself.

As I put the final element on the table, I paused and looked around. Flick tucked in first, breaking the ice so I could sit down and stop worrying about it.

Barely daring to breathe, I waited until they'd dished up everything and were eating before I took some for myself. Almost immediately they made happy noises, and I relaxed.

For the next twenty minutes I felt nothing but happiness. These few people had become my life in the city, some kind of a family that was beginning to feel comfortable. I still had a lot of questions and I worried about what I could do to sort out the anger and fear and antagonism I still got from a lot of the other dragons.

But for a while, it was gone from my head and I laughed and talked with friends and my new mentor. It was bliss.

"Did you cook before you came here?" Flick asked. "With Anthony or anything?"

"Sometimes, but rarely. Anthony liked to cook and I often used to not bother when there was just me."

"Wasted talent," he replied.

"Anthony would have said it was a hidden talent. That they were the best kind when they emerged, because it is like a flower blooming to see the sun for the first time." Ben's eyes went wide as soon as he finished speaking, and I almost dropped my fork as it was partway to my mouth.

We looked at each other and silence fell as everyone stared at us.

"Did someone say something?" Neritas asked.

"Just a memory of Anthony that we both share," I replied, trying to deflect a little. "Sometimes we both have similar memories but they happened at different times and it reminds us that he let us both see the real him."

This seemed to satisfy my friends, who continued to eat and ask me questions about what I'd made and why. Conversation soon turned to classes and what we were all learning, and to Ben and how he felt being an honorary dad for a while.

It was fun to tease him a little, and it took the pressure off me to focus on someone else. A part of me couldn't wait for everyone to leave, however. Ben had found another possible key phrase for us to use with the journal, and I wanted to know what the next pages said.

My friends had other plans, however, and suggested we play board games, then asked me to go with them to watch the meteors that should be passing over.

"Go," Ben said when I hesitated. "It will do you some good. Anything else can wait. No matter how important it is."

Although I knew what he was trying to tell me, I noticed Neritas raise an eyebrow slightly as he also caught the double meaning of Ben's words. If he thought something was strange about the way Ben encouraged me, he didn't comment, however.

I went with the others, grateful to have three friends with me and to finally be settling into the city a little. We went down to the shore on one side of the city, the sound of the waves almost instantly soothing.

At first I worried and shied away from even the shadows of other dragons, in either form. But it was as if the dark helped to lend me anonymity, and everyone else had other places to be.

After the first few times I'd been harassed on my way around the city, I had deliberately avoided being out at night and made sure I was only going places when my two protectors were around. Knowing they were also changing their lives and what they would normally do so that they could help provide some safety for me, I didn't feel as if I could ask them to guard me in the evenings. Especially when Ben was always around and it was easier to just stay with him.

Eventually, we were sitting down on the pebbly sand, looking up at the clear sky and all the stars. Although lights shone in the city, they were dim enough that they didn't stop us from being able to see the tiny pinpricks of light.

"Do you think your next flying lesson will be as eventful as last week?" Flick asked when we'd been sitting in silence for a minute or two.

"I hope not," I answered without thinking.

"You made them all so envious," Tiffany replied. "Several dragons have barely talked about anything else since."

"Really? I just flew."

"Just flew?" Flick looked shocked. "You did something that even we find difficult. You're amazing up there. I'm hoping the next lesson is even more cool."

"So they can be more envious and more spiteful and I can risk my life yet again?" I asked, not sure I understood his delight.

"No. So they can realize that they can't keep up no matter how hard they try."

I tilted my head to the side, wondering if that was likely to happen or if it was wishful thinking on his behalf. Whatever it was I couldn't let it stop me becoming the best I could be.

It wasn't really something I wanted to think about now, however. After making food and having my new friends over for dinner, I was feeling good about life. I didn't want to be reminded about all the difficulties.

It seemed I wasn't going to get that luxury, however. We were still waiting for the main group of meteorites to show when more dragons came down. Even in the dark, I could tell it was at least one of the female dragons who had a problem with me.

My friends' reaction was even more of a giveaway. They all shifted closer to me. For the first time, I realized they had all sat protectively around me.

"Letting the freak get some fresh air, are we?" the girl called over. "Hope you've let her know that even she can't fly high enough to reach the meteors. Though she might do us all a favor and try."

I ignored her, used to keeping a straight face in front of bullies, but I noticed Neritas clench both fists. Trying to be subtle, I leaned forward to bring my mouth closer to his ear.

"Not worth it," I whispered. "It only makes it worse, unless you can make them wish they were never born to mess with you. And then you're just making them scared."

"And scared people are unpredictable."

"Exactly."

Thankfully the first larger meteor streaked across the sky and drew everyone's attention. They were stunning to watch and something I'd never seen before, so I did what everyone else did and tipped my head back and watched the sky.

There was something wonderful about enjoying a shared experience, talking in low voices while sitting there and watching the stars put on a display for us.

I lost track of time, feeling myself relax for the first time in a while.

The feeling only lasted so long, however, before I could have sworn someone was watching me. An uneasy feeling that I was under a microscope came over me.

Looking around, I tried to pinpoint if there was someone in one of the other groups staring at me. No matter how much I looked around, however, I couldn't see another dragon in any of the groups on the beach looking anywhere but up at the stars for more than a few seconds.

For now I was completely forgotten.

The watched feeling didn't go away, however.

"Something wrong?" Neritas asked. It drew the attention of Tiffany and Flick as well.

"I don't think so…maybe," I replied.

As I looked around again, now being studied by all of my friends, I felt the feeling get worse. It was almost as if someone was trying to get my attention. I looked back up the beach, pretty sure it was coming from that direction now that it was a more intense feeling. I thought of the splinter group and the cell phone I'd been given by Jace. Although I'd kept it with me all the time to begin with, the chaos of the evening had meant that I'd left it at the apartment.

"Stay here. Something is bugging me, but I don't want to spook anyone. If I'm not back in a couple of minutes, one of you come to find me."

Neritas reached up to grab my wrist as I stood.

"Are you sure about this? You shouldn't be going off alone."

"I have a feeling that this is something I need to do alone or it won't work." The moment I finished speaking I knew I'd said something strange, but Neritas studied me for only a few more seconds before he let me go.

"Ten minutes. Then I'm following as fast as I can, and I don't care who or what I scare."

I nodded, smiling at his protectiveness. Although there was an element to it that was annoying, it was also sweet of him to care so much.

Hoping that I wasn't wrong and that I could trust whatever was summoning me, I moved carefully up the beach. My movement drew me the odd glance from dragons in other groups, but none from my most ardent haters. For now I could move freely.

It was strange to even attempt to do so, but someone was watching me and possibly even trying to draw my attention, and I just couldn't wait among my friends to find out who and what they wanted.

Although I couldn't be sure exactly who, there was a part of me that had expectations and hopes. I wanted it to be a step toward my future. These thoughts kept running through my head as I grew more nervous and then reassured myself that this was what I wanted.

Eventually, I reached the edge of the cliff, a path winding upwards in one direction. Another forked off the first to run along the base of the cliffs. I wasn't sure which to take at first, but the latter stuck to the shadows, and the higher path curved around to the front entrance of the city.

I walked along the lower one, moving as silently as I could and listening for any signs that I might not be alone, ahead or behind. It was strange being somewhere by myself for the first time in weeks. With everything that had happened and how badly other dragons had reacted to having a red dragon in their midst, I had been escorted or accompanied everywhere, and when I was home, Ben had almost always been there.

With the desire to be by myself for a while hitting me like a ton of bricks, I considered lingering there for a while. Neritas would likely be following me soon, however.

Even if I wanted to, I couldn't be alone.

As much as I wanted to stop now, I couldn't. I had to keep going. Something was still nagging at me and I had to find out what.

I followed the path for a few more yards before a cave opened up on my left. It was dark, brooding, and I almost walked past it—but a light flashed very briefly and drew my attention to it.

When it flashed for the second time, I got the impression it was for me and I was meant to follow it. I was wary, but I didn't have the same uneasy feeling that I had when the shadow catchers were nearby.

Heading into the cave, I put out a hand and moved slower so I didn't trip. The cave wall was cool and smooth beneath my fingers.

As I rounded a natural corner in the cave, a small light flickered into being. A woman I recognized stood holding it in the palm of her hand. Jace.

"Hello, Scarlet. Are you ready for your first mission?"

"I guess that would depend on what it is, wouldn't it?" I replied, still wary.

"We just want information. It's pretty much all we want and all we'll ever want. We're hoping that you have the skills we need to acquire it, however."

"Okay, I'm vaguely interested. Give me what you've got."

The woman rummaged in a small briefcase that seemed to materialize from nowhere and pulled out a map with some coordinate markers on it, then she produced a piece of crumpled-up paper and handed it over.

"Our information is incomplete, but I hope this is enough to start with."

"Have you got a due date for this?" I didn't think I should agree to anything before I talked to Ben, but I might not have a choice.

There was also the pressing matter of knowing that another dragon was going to follow me if I was gone for too long, and this meeting wasn't proving quick yet. I needed to get the information I could and leave.

"No due date, but the sooner the better. We don't like to rush anything and put pressure on you, but all information helps."

"Got it. How do I get it to you?"

"Bring it back here and leave it in a watertight bag." As she spoke, she moved her light and pointed it at a small shelf on the cavern edge. "Put it here and we'll find it."

"Then what will happen?"

"We'll be in touch again. As always. It's better if we keep things simple and approach one task at a time."

I didn't argue. Not only did I get the impression that it would be a waste of my time no matter how good a reason I had, I didn't have time to do so now. Neritas would be looking for me now.

After saying goodbye and tucking the map and crumpled paper safely in my pockets, I made my way back to the entrance of the cave with the small amount of starlight I could see by.

It was easier returning, the clouds having moved and cleared some of the sky to give me a better idea of where I was heading. I saw Neritas coming my way, seeming to smell the route I took, and that encouraged me back even quicker.

"Everything all right?" he asked as soon as I was close enough that he could practically whisper it.

"Yes. I was worried it was something like a shadow catcher, but no, I think I was picking up on nothing and just being paranoid."

Neritas studied my face as if he didn't quite believe me, but he let it go and simply motioned for me to lead the way back to the others. I felt the weight of the extra items in my pockets as if they were a thousand times heavier and everyone would notice I had them.

Although I'd spent a few evenings sneaking around homes as a kid, nothing had ever felt like this. The knowledge that I was conspiring with an organization that was outlawed and banned from many places was dangerous in a way I didn't entirely comprehend.

All I knew was that I needed to take it all to Ben before I decided anything else.

CHAPTER ELEVEN

My stomach felt as if someone had tied it in knots. Ben had the information I'd been given on his desk and he was studying it far harder than I had. It was early in the morning. Neither of us had been able to sleep with this development.

"Was this all they gave you?" he asked eventually.

"Yes. And I didn't exactly have long to ask questions. She didn't want to talk much and I had my trio of guardians not far away."

The corner of Ben's mouth flicked up at the mention of my friends. One of them, he'd met for the first time yesterday evening, and he'd only exchanged a few words with the other two in the past. It had been good to introduce them all a bit more.

Although I wasn't the most social of people, I was getting used to having them around—until a situation like last night, when someone from an outlawed terrorist group came to ask me to help them get information. Then it was a little awkward.

I had wondered about telling my friends. It certainly would make things easier. But there was a good chance that at least one of the three would feel the need to report me or something.

"Okay, I think we should follow this lead as best we can and as soon as we can. It looks like they want us to either go talk to someone or go get some paperwork on a guy's finances. Someone linked to the dragon world but potentially not a dragon."

I'd reached a similar conclusion but hadn't wanted to say anything while Ben was still processing. Although Anthony had wanted the two of us to work together a lot, and we definitely needed to translate his journal with our combined mind, everything else seemed to be up to one or the other of us.

"This is interesting."

"How so?" I asked, surprised by the addition.

"The journal entries we translated last night thanks to that conversation with your friends. It's all about how this organization can seem like they're up to one thing when they're up to another, but that they appear to have good intentions."

"That's…cryptic."

Ben sat back and looked at me. "What do you think this information they asked for could be related to?"

"I have no idea. And it's just information. How bad can it be?"

"Information can be very valuable in the right hands. Or the wrong ones." Ben frowned before his expression went more neutral. "I think we need to be careful, but I still think we should proceed."

"Want to get copies of the things we find so that we have it too?" I asked.

"I'm not sure it's going to be anything we can use or understand, necessarily," he replied. "I think we'll have to conduct a little research of our own. Assuming this isn't the only thing they ever ask us to do."

"Then we have a plan, and I'm sure that with plenty of brains, some leeway from the city elders in keeping us here, and a car, we can get it done and sorted."

Ben didn't look so convinced, but he got up anyway.

"I think the hardest part of all our challenges is going to be getting out of the city. I've taken you out twice already in only a few weeks. To take you out again when we're not sure how long it's going to take, exactly where we're going, and what appearance people are already judging us on…"

"Are you saying you think people are wondering if we might be a couple?" I asked, not sure I'd followed everything Ben meant by his words.

"We are sharing an apartment and you do spend a lot of time alone with me. On top of that, you have two of the city's most desired bachelor dragons following you around everywhere and you've not hooked up with either of them. I'm pretty sure you have the entire population talking about who you might be in a relationship with."

"No one has even so much as asked."

"Perhaps not, but those two are with you everywhere for a reason. And honestly, having now been a sort-of parent for a little while, I'm beginning to wonder what their intentions toward you are and why you're not interested in one or the other of them."

"You've been my parental figure for less than three

weeks." I grinned and noticed he was as well. This was becoming a silly conversation. A tease about my level of interest in my friends.

"Has it really only been that long?" Ben suddenly looked haunted and glanced at Anthony's journal. I understood all too well the change in his mood. We both missed Anthony, and now and then something was said or done that brought his absence back. It hurt, and only time would allow us to heal and recover enough so that it wouldn't.

"Tell the folks in charge that I need to clear out my apartment now that I'm not going back. That it's not worth the cost when I'm finally settling here and being accepted."

Ben raised an eyebrow and looked at me. "You know we'd actually have to do that or it would look weird?"

I nodded. If my excuse worked, I would have to actually let go of my apartment and there would be nowhere else for me to go to but back here to the dragon city. But Anthony's apartment was empty still. Of course, his had come with his job, and at some point a permanent caretaker would take it on again.

We tried to think of something else, but we both knew it wasn't an option and that meant we had to continue with this plan instead.

"All right. Pack up some stuff. Whatever you think you'll need. I'm going to go speak to the elders before the day gets too late and they're difficult to pin down."

I watched Ben go and tried to think of more I could do, but for now we had to follow the path laid out before us and hope that it was the right course of action.

By the time he came back, I was ready to go. I'd told Neritas and Flick to go on to classes without me for now, and neither of them had liked it much, but they'd left me in peace.

"Did we succeed?" I asked.

"Sort of. They're not happy about it and want us to check in regularly. We're definitely going to need to actually do what we're saying we will on top of this side mission, though."

It was what we'd expected, but I felt a pang of sadness nonetheless. I'd lived in that apartment as the first home of my own for my entire adult life so far, and letting go of it was going to be hard. None of my life was ever going to be the same again, however, and I'd come to accept that. It was time for me to let go and move on.

Within ten minutes we were in the car and driving out of the city. Once more, the woman guarding the city border, Capricia, with her array of black dragons, had given us a hard time, but she still seemed to hold a sort of begrudging respect for me.

Being out of the city gave me a familiar feeling of relief in some ways. I didn't have to worry about other dragons attacking me. And while we were in the car and going between places, I didn't have to worry about shadow catchers either.

But my destination wasn't entirely safe anymore. And I had a mission that could require me to do all sorts of dangerous things. This wasn't about to be an easy day or two.

We discussed the plan to get the information and clear out my apartment. Thankfully, I was a fairly clean person and there wasn't much to do beyond pack the rest of my life into boxes and load things into a vehicle. A lot of the big, bulky furniture was going to have to go or be sold. There was nowhere for it in the dragon city, even if I did want to keep it.

We needed to know what was at the coordinates I'd been given, and what kind of place might have the financial records the group was looking for.

Ben drove close to the first one, and we kept our eyes out for something that might feel right. In the end, we found ourselves in a rundown neighborhood, the area made up of a little section with a convenience store, a nightclub, dentist, and an accountant's office. They'd all set up in old houses.

I was relieved when it was all that we found nearby so we could be sure that the accountant was our goal. Now we'd seen a bit more and had more information, I pulled out the crumpled piece of paper that had come with the map.

On it was a name, a social security number, and a string of letters, numbers, and symbols with uppercase and lowercase letters. It looked like some kind of randomly generated password, but if it was, then that meant that I was being expected to hack into something.

No part of me liked the idea. I wasn't a hacker.

"I think we should come back when it's closed," Ben said. "Scope out the place and then break in."

"Why should we break in when we could get what we need legally?" I asked, confused by his rush to go straight to crime.

"If you think you can get what you need from this place without committing a crime or getting a lawyer involved, be my guest," Ben replied, motioning for me to get out of the car as he pulled over.

"Wish me luck or something." I stormed off out of the car and acted like it was the end of the world.

I heard Ben chuckle after me as I started to focus on what I needed to do. Somewhere in the building ahead was the information this message was asking for. Now all I had to do was go and claim it. Even though it wasn't mine or his.

I paused at the door, trying to work out what to say. In the end I decided to stay as close to the truth as I possibly could. I walked into the building with the piece of paper in hand, making sure it was crumpled enough that no one else could read it.

There was a woman at the desk ahead and she looked to be very busy putting some kind of document together that had the pages all muddled up, un-numbered. As soon as she noticed me she put her work down. Almost immediately, I wished that she'd not seen me as a customer and I'd been able to walk around.

"Can I help you?" she asked.

"Possibly. I'm trying to track down an old family friend. He's someone who was once part of my life and did some lovely things for me when I was growing up. I want to repay him if I can."

As I spoke, the receptionist's eyebrows lifted slowly. This was clearly not an inquiry she was expecting.

"I know it's very strange, but the only thing I remember about him is that someone here used to do his taxes. I was hoping that I could get an address or something. Some way of contacting him. Maybe even just leave him a message."

The receptionist had no clue how to deal with my request, and decided to get someone a little higher up in the chain of command. It was a very good thing she did, because I wasn't sure how much more I could have added to the lie I was telling.

If nothing else, I wanted to verify that the records of the person we were looking for were at least in the building, even if I had to come back later to break in for them.

I repeated the story to a graying accountant with a paunch.

Almost immediately he frowned. "That's not an easy request to meet."

"I know. I'm sorry, I wish I wasn't having to ask like this, but he was so kind to me and I just want to let him know that he changed the course of my life for the better, and I've got no other way."

The guy lifted his hand to show me he understood and didn't want me to keep talking. I thought maybe I'd laid it on too thick, but he beckoned for me to follow him.

"I don't know what I can give you, but I can at least help you figure some stuff out and confirm what you know."

I exhaled in genuine relief as he led me through to an archive room and I gave him the name again. It was strange to stand there and watch a guy find me the information I needed without realizing why I truly needed it.

I felt bad that I was manipulating someone's kindness, but with any luck this would never get back to the accountant at all. He was just making it easier for me to pass on information. Hopefully it wouldn't ever put anyone in danger.

Although I tried to look relaxed, I paid attention to the

file the accountant went to, and where exactly it was in the room.

"Can you confirm the name again?" the accountant asked before he would even properly pull the file from the case.

I repeated it, grateful I could remember it from the piece of paper and didn't need to read it. That wouldn't help at all if I was to persuade this man that I really knew my target.

"Okay, let me see what I've got."

He opened the file but kept it tilted away from me and I got the impression that no matter how much I persuaded him to give me something to go on, I wasn't going to get to see the files I needed. No matter how I played this, I was going to have to come back and break in when everyone was gone home for the night.

CHAPTER TWELVE

Exhausted from even ten minutes of being grilled and having to think on my feet, I exhaled with relief once more when I stepped out of the accountant's. I hadn't succeeded, and it was obvious on my face as I went back to Ben and the car.

"I was about to come in and look for you." Ben pointed to an alley down the street.

Lingering at the side of it, looking around and sniffing, was a shadow catcher. It was only as I saw it that I realized I had been so nervous and preoccupied with lying that I'd not noticed the mental warning of the vile creatures approaching. There were two, and it appeared as if they were hunting me out.

"Do you think they can feel me the way I feel them?" I asked as Ben slowly pulled away, careful to keep us as quiet as possible.

"Maybe when they get close. But they would have to have hundreds through this city to be able to find you everywhere they have. And in the woods. No, something or someone is directing them to you somehow."

"But no one but you and I know we're here today."

"The contact from this terrorist group knows, and anyone else they've told."

I gulped, not liking what that meant. I thought back to the last few meetings, though. The person I'd spoken to each time had appeared to be at least as surprised as I was when the shadow catchers did appear. If someone on their side of dealings was talking, it wasn't the people I was meeting face to face.

Thankfully, this time we could drive away and put distance between us and the shadow catchers.

Ben didn't want to head back to my apartment. "Let's get some food and plan how to get these files. I want to make sure we're not risking a safe place we might need at some point. At least while it's still ours to use."

"I wouldn't exactly call it safe. It's a place that others know is mine. I'm already surprised that the shadow catchers haven't shown up there when they made it to Anthony's apartment." Only now did I process how scared that made me, when I wanted to be brave and face anything coming at me head-on.

"You aren't the only one who has had that thought." Ben kept his gaze on the road, but I saw him set his jaw.

We rode in silence to a drive-through fast-food joint and picked up enough for both of us for now and extra to keep us going through the night. It was junk food, but after the food in the city, it was a nice change.

As we ate, I told Ben what had happened and what I'd learned about the inside of the accountant's office.

"Looks like we're going to be attempting some breaking and entering then," Ben proposed as I finished.

For a few seconds I couldn't think, eat, or respond. Was I really considering this? So far, we hadn't really broken any moral laws in my head. We had broken into Anthony's possessions but we hadn't done any harm and we had been the ones they were intended for. Morally, I hadn't felt guilty.

This, however, was very different. I could be putting something or someone in danger, and I was definitely taking something I had no right to for reasons I wasn't aware of.

"I'm not sure about this," I said out loud when I couldn't find a way of justifying it in my head.

"I'd be worried if you were," Ben replied. "This isn't something to be considered lightly. And I'm not entirely okay with it either. But for some reason, this was the sort of thing that Anthony did for these people. And he thought it was important and their reasons were solid enough that he put it in his journal to ask me to trust this part of the process and you, and to know that it does have a good purpose beyond the intentions of this organization."

"The journal said that?"

"Yes. The latest entry. It specifically told me to trust you, trust their process, but to make sure that I was aware of as much as possible."

"As in pay attention to the information we're getting for them?" I already wondered what that financial information might reveal and if it was something I could make heads or tails of.

"I believe that's what Anthony meant." Ben started the

engine again. We'd finished eating, and enough time had passed that the accountant's office was likely to be shut or almost empty by now.

I felt my body tense and my blood go cold at the thought of what I was about to do. I'd learned how to pick locks, but I'd only ever done it in the past for good reasons too.

"Do you want me to do this?" Ben asked when we pulled up outside the office. We were far enough away that someone on the reception desk wouldn't necessarily see our car or notice us, but close enough that we could see there was a light still on in one of the rooms.

I shook my head. There was no way I was going to ask Ben to do this. The group we were liaising with seemed to want to deal with me, and I didn't want to get Ben in trouble if this went wrong. He had already made it clear how he felt and that he was only doing this for my sake. And no matter what happened, I didn't want him to lose his home in Detaris. If this went wrong, I would take the blame entirely. In my mind, it was the only possible way.

Despite my willingness to be the one to break in and steal, I wasn't going to do so while someone was still there and might hear me.

"It might be best that you do it while they're there," Ben replied when I told him. "Because if they have an alarm system, it won't yet be active, and people are going to be less suspicious of someone trying to get into a building that isn't empty."

Although I hated to admit it, Ben had a really good point. This wasn't ideal, but it was probably the most safe way to get the information.

I took a deep breath, opened the car door and got out. The shadow catchers that had been here earlier didn't seem to be here any longer, but I didn't intend to be caught out a second time.

As I walked closer to the building, I reached into the bag I had on my shoulder and pulled out the tools I thought would be best for the job. I had a set of tools for picking a lock, but the door had one more element that would make it harder to get inside.

There was a bolt that came across to hold an internal door shut. The accountant had scanned his pass on an electronic touch pad right beside it. He'd also punched in a code, so that may present a bigger problem, but even those sorts of doors could be forced.

Outside, however, I just needed to pick the lock.

Thankfully, we were in a quiet part of the city and it was already late enough that there were very few people around. I still didn't crouch by the front door, however. I didn't want to look obvious. Instead, I walked up like I was putting an actual key in the lock. It took me a few jiggles and a moment of sheer panic when a car drove past, but eventually I felt it click and I turned the handle.

Within seconds, I was inside. I paused, my heart racing. This was a lot worse than I'd thought. My hands were starting to shake, and my head felt fuzzy from the lack of oxygen getting to my brain.

I wanted to give my body a chance to rest, but I couldn't linger. At any point the person still in their office could decide that they were done for the day and come to lock up.

Moving toward the next door, I pulled open the strange

tool I had. It was hopefully going to slide between the door and the wall and help me get the area open, but I had only used it once and I hadn't had much success with it.

Not that I had intended on telling Ben about that. As far as I was concerned, that wasn't something he needed to know. It would only worry him.

Taking a few deep breaths to steady my hands and focus myself, I tried to work the door open while making as little noise as possible.

I was in very little danger of being seen unless the other occupant of the building came to leave. It helped me stay on task and stay calmer, although the longer I tried to get the door open, the more nervous I got.

It took me almost five minutes, but eventually I managed to get the door bolt moved and my stick through the gap enough that it would stop the door lock from engaging again.

Despite doing everything as quietly and as carefully as possible, I was cautious as I pulled the door open and looked beyond. The office still in use was near one end of the corridor, and I wanted a back room that came off a T junction at the other end. As long as I was quiet enough, I was fairly sure I'd get away with it.

I moved as slowly as I dared along the route the accountant had taken me earlier in the day. I paused outside a room that was the same number of doors down as I'd counted this afternoon.

The door beside it felt more like the right door, however, and it threw me. There was something about it that looked right when the first one I'd stopped in front of didn't.

Eventually, I decided to trust my instinct and opened the second door. Following my gut had always been something I preferred to do.

I was right. The racks of labeled files looked familiar enough that I could hurry inside, close the door behind me and go to the right section of the room. Within a few minutes I had the guy's files up and I was able to look through the financial records.

It hadn't been specified that I get the information in a particular way, so I took my phone out and took a picture. If I had been in a hurry or somewhere else, I might have tried to find a way of getting the documents in another form. As it was, I was in a rush, and photos meant I could also look at all the information at a later date.

It was only as I was taking the tenth photo that I realized this was information about repeated payments into a fund of some kind. This person had put a lot of money into an account or given a lot to another for a significant length of time. It wasn't a small amount, and it went back many years.

By the time I had all the pictures of this element, I remembered the other things that my contacts had requested. I wasn't entirely sure where they were. There hadn't been a need to find them earlier in the day, and I wasn't practiced enough at any of this information-gathering stuff to know how to do it effectively.

Looking through the file, I tried to work out what else I needed. I realized there were more documents about what this guy was paying for. I couldn't help it. I read some of them, wondering what he was so devoted to.

As I read down further, I found myself getting chills.

He'd been paying into a fund, indeed, and the recipient had begun to draw from it on her seventeenth birthday. It listed the first payment to her and how it would hopefully continue to grow the principal so she could draw more in the long run.

What made me pause, however, was the amount of the first payment to the fund recipient. It was the exact amount I had been given from a fund by an anonymous benefactor.

Was this even possible? Had I been asked to go get information on my own benefactor? Did the group I was working for know this? Was this some way of showing me that they knew stuff about me no one else did?

I had no way of knowing, so I continued to take photos, getting all the information that might be useful for me as well. It felt like it took ages, and I hoped it wasn't anything that was going to get whoever this person was in trouble. If they were truly the one behind my fund and helping me live, then I owed them for a lot of meals and general survival. Of course, it could have been a coincidence, and I had to remain calm and level headed until I knew for sure.

With all the information I wanted finally stowed on my phone, I tucked the device deep between two layers of clothes so they couldn't easily take it off me if I got caught, and made my way back to the room door.

I paused again and listened to see if I could work out where the accountant was and if they planned to leave any time soon.

I assumed the coast was clear and I was on my own, and headed down the hallway back to the front door. Partway there I felt the unmistakable feeling of another creature nearby. The shadow catchers were back. Swearing under my breath, I hurried along faster toward the door. This was going from bad to worse.

With the middle door already propped open, I retrieved my stick and let it close as if it had never been opened. I hurried to the outside door and pulled it open, wondering if the alarm was going to go off, but it didn't and I was soon outside in the dark evening air and heading back to Ben.

As soon as he saw me, he drove the car from his parking space, but there was a shadow catcher closer and they reacted fast to my presence.

"Frelling gooseberries," I murmured as I ran in the opposite direction.

The shadow catcher hurried along the pavement behind me, letting out the strange screeching noise they often did. It made my blood run cold as I heard it catching up to me, but I didn't stop running.

At the next junction, Ben pulled the car across the road and flung open the passenger door for me. I dove into the car and he put his foot down before I could even close the door.

I exhaled with relief as I closed it and sat myself up properly.

"They really seem to be drawn to you," Ben observed. "And I'm starting to worry that someone is following us or somehow knows what our every move outside the city is."

I didn't doubt that Ben was right, and it made me angry and tired. Either way, it was time to get somewhere more suitable for both of us.

CHAPTER THIRTEEN

We drove in silence most of the way back toward the city. The shadow catchers in my way yet again were starting to make me feel really worried. Something wasn't adding up, and something wasn't right about the group I was working for either.

"I think I want to hand this information over as quickly as I can possibly do so and still be acting sensibly," I told Ben as the cliffs the city sat on came into view.

"In that cave?" He was one of only a few people who knew there was something there of any significance.

"That's all I've got to go on. She implied a whole heap of things, but she was also really vague. I don't have a better guess."

"It's okay." Ben reached out for me, picking up on the irritation I felt. "We'll find a way to figure out what is going on and maybe deter a bunch of these shadow catchers along the way. You seem to be able to put them off when you combine your powers with mine and those of a black dragon."

"Something like that. I imagine a lot of dragons never get close enough to a shadow catcher to find out if they can do anything to stop them," I replied. Although I was a red dragon and that made me special, I really didn't like thinking of myself as more important than anyone else.

"Maybe once this is done I'll be able to sleep and leave all the defending to someone else. Even if only for one night here and there."

"You act like the universe is making it impossible for you to do anything. You have a safe space among friends. Someone once told me that you can't enjoy the here and now if you're constantly striving to be better tomorrow. And you don't make friends long term by pretending to be something you're not comfortable with either."

I tried to think of a suitable response to Ben, but the truth was, I wasn't sure I wanted to go to the effort to fit in and start again. I didn't actually want to put a bunch of effort into friend making. I wanted to be the right person for the right job and for people to always find it easy to like me, and to be respected.

Of course, life and social interactions didn't work like that. Some people weren't reasonable and decided they hated you based on appearances or worse.

"Go past the city," I suggested when Ben came close to the entrance. "I don't want to go back yet. They make it so difficult to get away again."

"We haven't been able to empty your apartment yet, so we'd have good reason to make another trip, but I agree. For now, let's stay out. We'll need to prepare copies of all the information you've gathered anyway."

Ben continued along the winding path until there was

somewhere he could pull over in the dead of night and remain hidden and both of us could walk down to the beach and caves once we were done making copies of the photos I'd taken.

I took my time, using Ben's laptop to back up the photos from my phone and add the ones I thought the group wanted to a thumb drive. I didn't give them everything, wanting to keep a little of the information to myself, but I gave them what I thought would be enough to confirm anything they were looking to confirm.

It was strange to have Ben with me this time, when the last time I'd wandered off by myself and left all my friends behind. I had enjoyed the moment alone then, but there was something about having Ben with me this time that was comforting. And on top of being the company I needed, he'd brought the extra food we'd bought at the drive-through.

We left his laptop in the car and made our way into the cave and looked around for the drop-off point. Eventually Ben spotted the shelf where I had been asked to put the information.

After doing so, I flopped down and tried to decide if I wanted to eat now or save it for later. There was no way to know how long it would take for someone to come pick up the thumb drive or if they would be put off by me sticking around and having Ben with me. I hoped that wasn't the case, as I didn't want to waste my time or theirs.

In the end Ben decided for me, sitting down nearby and pulling out the extra burgers and fries. At the same time, I used the cell phone I'd been given to message Jace.

"We should keep our strength up and be aware of any

approaching danger. There's only one way in and out of these caves and I don't like being trapped by shadow catchers."

"Even when you know I can rebuff them and hurt them somehow?" I asked, surprised at Ben's sudden cautiousness.

"Don't get me wrong. There's a huge advantage to everything you can do. But let's not tempt fate. At some point it decides to screw you."

"That's optimistic of you," I replied, but I understood his sentiment. Sometimes it wasn't worth tempting fate and sometimes it was. It didn't matter today, though. We were going to sit there together and let everything fall the way it would.

We waited for what seemed like hours, neither of us doing much but getting up to wander now and then. A few times I went to the entrance to the cave and felt around for shadow catchers. None of them seemed to be close, however, and the general relief that I didn't always attract them within a few minutes was comforting.

Of course, I still had no contact, and once more I found myself wondering if I'd made the right choices recently or not.

Finally, I heard the approach of someone else.

Jace came into view. As soon as she saw me she frowned.

"You seem to have a knack for getting yourself in a lot of trouble and then showing off while getting away with it. Are there any more of those vile creatures around? They seem to hound you wherever you go."

"There aren't any right now, but yes, for some reason they sense me, and I wish they wouldn't."

The woman came closer, studying me in the dragon light and appearing to find something she liked the look of.

"What did you find for me?" she asked.

"It took me a while to work out how to get access to the records you wanted, but I got there in the end." I folded my arms across my chest. "It's in the cave. Ben is watching it all."

"Noted." Jace went to walk past me but I was still mostly in her way.

"Let me show you." I suddenly felt protective over Ben. I also didn't want her to just waltz in and make any judgment calls. And I definitely wanted to see her reaction to the information we'd gathered. Not that I expected her to necessarily look as soon as she got it, but there was a chance and it made me curious.

She glanced at the first picture I pulled up on my phone and confirmed it was financial information about the man she wanted. "Thank you. It means a lot to us that you did this so well and so fast. I hope I can repay you soon with something you need. I must go now, however, and—"

I lifted a hand, cutting her off as I realized I felt a strange uneasy presence in the back of my mind.

With growing fear, I quickly identified the aura of some shadow catchers. I didn't waste time in telling them.

Jace's eyes went wide. "Again, while you're around?"

"I could say the same to you, if you're throwing accusations about what they're doing here." It was a little unfair of me, but I was equally surprised by the sheer mass of the vile demons and what they wanted with me.

"Now isn't the time to ask why they're here," Ben pointed out. "We need to get out of these caves before they block us in."

Ben was correct and I had every intention of obeying him. Getting out and away from the shadow catchers was the first step.

"We need to get out onto the beach and into the water," I said, lowering my voice in case it carried through the cave network as well.

I took the lead, aware that I was the one with the most confidence today. I was also the one most aware of the shadow catchers' positions. It made sense.

Jace appeared to still be angry, but I noticed that she made sure the information was safe as she trudged after me. I created the faintest of lights with my bare hand and tried to make sure it would guide everyone.

The shadow catchers moved fast along the cliff base, however, and we were still stumbling through the front part of the cave when they came around a small corner and one of them stopped across the cavern entrance.

"This isn't good," Jace commented as she almost bumped into the back of me.

"No shit, Sherlock." I took several steps back. So far the shadow catchers seemed to be lingering, like I had been, but that would change if they thought they detected me.

Ben gently took my arm and guided me backward. I was grateful for his presence—at least one of my companions would stand by me. I wouldn't be facing the terrifying beasts alone.

There was nowhere to go but deeper into the caves to look for a way to hide or sneak past it, hopefully without getting too close and definitely not letting the shadow catchers know that we were there. Something far easier said than done.

Jace struggled to keep up as I led the way, feeling the shadow catchers enter the place, where they at least had a lot of confusing smells to try to decipher. It didn't help much when we were all trying to get out of the caves all in silence.

Eventually I managed to get us to a much larger cavern within the cave network, my mind always working hard to save myself. Making it very dark, I hid us in the shadows until I felt Jace reaching out for me. Realizing the touch was her way of trying to apologize and be nice, I wasn't sure how to respond.

I gave her hand a squeeze and whispered for both of them to stay close and try not to make a sound.

They didn't reply, but squeezed a hand each.

The next few minutes were some of the hardest of my life. Once more I had to hold still while the enemy came to me.

Two shadow catchers entered the room, following our scent trail. We had moved around the large cavern in a clockwise pattern and the pair of shadow catchers were following that route. It was one of the few ways that shadow catchers were predictable that could be used against them without them even realizing.

Having creatures that were almost entirely blind and relied on scent and hearing made a difference to our escape plans. Knowing they could see a little had given me another advantage. I could temporarily blind and disorient them by shining very brightly.

Slowly, I led my friends from the cave, feeling forward with my feet and the small amount of light I dared to create as we snuck around behind the shadow catchers and kept moving toward the entrance.

A couple of times, we came closer to the creatures as they headed deeper into the caves, following the path I'd taken in looking for the drop-off point, but we stayed ahead of them despite them gaining on the scented trail I'd left. My heart hammered so loudly in my chest I was sure that everyone should be able to hear it. Somehow the strategy of avoiding them and taking every opportunity to sneak out of the caves worked, however, and we made our way back out and onto the beach again. Only once we were safe outside and heading toward the water did I dare to make more noise.

"We need to get into the water and walk along the beach front for half a mile or so away from the city," Ben whispered.

I remembered that shadow catchers couldn't go out on the water and it would also mask our scent. It was the safest way to get away from them, but I worried that they were going to put people in the city in danger.

"Both of you do that. I'm going to lead them away from the city and then I'll join you in the water," I replied.

Ben reached out to grab my hand and stop me, but I shook my head.

"I know you worry about me, but we both know that I have to do this. They can't find the city or dragons could die."

"For acting like there's nothing going on and keeping

everyone in the dark, there's a few elders who deserve to die," Jace replied, the disdain in her statement clear.

"Whether that's true or not, I think we both know that it wouldn't be the elders who'd get killed but some of the younger dragons who know only what they've been taught. I couldn't let them be harmed because of the mistakes of others."

Jace nodded and Ben squeezed the hand he'd grabbed hold of before relinquishing it.

"I'll help you. They might be following you for some reason, but you're right, and I know that you can do more to defend yourself if I'm there too."

As Ben finished speaking, he looked at Jace and she flicked her gaze between us a couple of times.

"Oh hell, the two of you will be the death of me at this rate, but consider me in as well."

I grinned as the three of us took off up the beach, running and no longer trying to be quiet. It was time to be the prey of a couple of shadow catchers for a while.

Although I'd felt afraid in the cave and tense, now I felt a strange sense of purpose along with it. My heart still raced and I'd have been a fool not to fear the monstrous creatures, but I wasn't running because of it. This time I had a more noble purpose and it felt good.

We made our way along the cliff path away from the city at first, the ground underfoot more firm there and easier to move along, but it soon tapered out and we were running on sand.

"We need to head into the woods and away from the water so we can lead them in a circle to the water," I called back as we ran.

I felt the shadow catchers behind us. They were slowly catching up, and we couldn't run forever.

"There's a stream another quarter mile up ahead. Not massive, but if we run away from the coast before it and then find it in the woods, they will hopefully think we've gone away from the beach." Jace panted as she spoke. I appreciated her knowledge of the terrain and her quick thinking, and I motioned for her to lead the way.

She hurried off, giving our mini train a new lease of life and speed. My body ached and I felt the beginnings of a stitch, but I wasn't about to give up. The people in the city needed me and I wanted to make sure they were safe. That meant running as hard as I could.

Despite the new-found enthusiasm, the shadow catchers moved faster than we could over sand, and we soon tired again. They were gaining on us, and I felt them like a strange weight in the back of my mind. A pressure that wouldn't go away or get easier.

I was also pretty sure that this close they could feel me a little. The pair made a few strange squawking noises. Although they had been close in the caves and they were further away now, it was as if this was somehow different. No matter how much farther we ran into the woods, there didn't seem to be any stream or river that would help us get away.

CHAPTER FOURTEEN

My lungs were burning and my side ached with the most painful stitch. The shadow catchers were now close enough that we could hear their pursuit and they didn't need our scent trail to follow us.

I wanted to demand Jace tell me where the stream was, but I saw her gasping for air. She either had hoped to reach it sooner or was struggling just as much to get us there. Given I had volunteered for this mission and both of them had joined me in the attempt to save the dragons in the city, I couldn't be angry at her.

Despite that, I wanted to be. These creatures got close to me far too often. And I didn't seem to be managing to fight them off anywhere nearly as easily as I felt I ought to be able to. I still knew so little about them.

Finally, the stream came into view, but a glance behind showed that we only had a hundred yards or so on the shadow catchers, and they could outrun all three of us. Our plan had also put us among the trees once more, so we couldn't take dragon form and fly without considerable risk.

This was a mess, and I'd got us into it.

Jace splashed into the stream, kicking up even more noise, and then she stopped. At first I wondered what she was doing and if she was going mad, but she put her finger to her lips and then slowly started to move downstream.

As soon as I joined her and went quiet as well, Ben reached for my hand and pulled me close.

"Make it dark," he whispered in my ear, his breath so light I struggled to work out what he'd said at first.

I could have hit myself for not thinking of the idea myself, but I quickly made it very dark as the shadow catchers continued to gain on us. At the same time we all walked at a snail's pace downstream, none of us lifting our feet out of the cold water.

Once more the shadow catchers came close to us and we had to move incredibly slowly past them while doing everything we could to not be detected.

The darkness seemed to help once more. The shadow catchers appeared to calm as they entered the darkened area. I wasn't sure if it soothed them, but there was a definite difference in their behavior.

As the shadow catchers reached the stream, they stopped and sniffed around the banks, and I continued to back up and away from them, Ben and Jace guiding me as I kept the dark stable and didn't take my eyes off the shadow catchers.

In my head, I willed them to try going the other way, up the stream. To assume that was the way we wanted to keep running because we'd come out this far, away from the sea.

They were either hearing me and deciding to mess with my thoughts or were much smarter than I'd given them credit for. They split up, one going upstream and the other coming downstream toward us.

I was immediately filled with fear and I almost froze to the spot. There was no way we could outrun a shadow catcher, and the stream wasn't wide enough to stop it reaching us from the shore. We were in big trouble.

Jace and Ben encouraged me to hurry. We still had twenty yards or so between us and the monster. I did my best to focus on just moving, trying to calm my erratic heart and my fears as they raced through my head.

Ben grabbed a branch from a nearby tree and broke it off. The shadow catcher closest heard the noise and came hurrying even faster.

He thrust it into one hand and grabbed Jace with the other before she could run away.

"Use it like a sword," he said to me. "Just like the guard shields."

"But they were holding them," I whispered back. Jace was trying to pull away, probably thinking we were mad.

"Grab her. She can funnel our powers," Ben told Jace. "Trust us, please. Or we're all dead."

Jace looked as if she was still considering running instead, her eyes wide and her head shaking, but I reached back and grabbed her other arm and turned to face the shadow catcher rushing straight at me.

I activated my powers, feeling the wave rushing into me from Ben and Jace as well, and then, to my surprise, they funneled into the wooden branch I held. As the shadow catcher lunged forward and right at me, the wood flashed brightly and seemed to supercharge.

Instead of decaying as everything usually did on contact with one of the monsters, the branch impaled it, as if the wood was a steel sword and the monster nothing more than a glob of soft flesh.

There was a gasp from somewhere behind me as I thrust again and the creature let out two loud shrieks and halted on the bank of the stream.

"How did you do that?" Jace demanded.

"Red dragon skill. As far as we can tell. I think it requires a blue dragon, a black dragon and me. I thought it would only work on the shields the guards of the city carry, but it turns out that I'm wrong."

"I'm glad that you are," Jace replied as the monster pulled back and we could move down the river, away from the badly injured shadow catcher.

The other one had heard the cries of pain, but it either didn't care or was too determined to see its option through for a set distance. It carried on upstream, away from us, though that was no surprise. The injured shadow catchers always seemed to back off.

For now we were safe, but we had to carry on putting distance between us and them, just in case. It was only as I turned and shrouded us in darkness again that I realized the stick I was holding was burned to a crisp.

I considered dropping it, but it brought me a strange sort of comfort, so I kept it in my grip and carried on. Despite needing to be quiet, we moved a little swifter, allowed a little more noise, and focused on increasing the distance between us and the monsters.

Jace seemed to have accepted my explanation and didn't say anything, choosing to stay focused on our opportunity to get away.

For the next ten minutes the shadow catcher presence receded in my head and we continued to the beach. Although the stream shallowed out as it ran across the sand and joined the water, we followed its course until we were ankle deep in the ocean. My feet were so cold they were beginning to hurt, but I wasn't going to complain. It had helped save our lives.

"Thank you," Jace said. "For the information and for... everything that followed. I've never seen anything quite like it, but I think I understand some of the stories about red dragons now. You have a gift and I can understand why Anthony protected you. Our organization may trade in information and have rules, but you have my support in any way I am capable of giving it in the future."

"Then I can only thank you. And hope that you'll remember that I retrieved this information in return for my own," I replied.

"I shall make sure that the request is granted as soon as it's possible to do so. You have to understand that what you're asking may not be something that we have the ability to find right away, but when we do, we'll leave it in the same place in the same cave."

"That should be enough."

I watched Jace walk away. She had the sense to go north through the water and not back toward the city or straight inland.

Ben frowned. "Well, that was a mess of a mission from start to finish."

"You're angry about it?" I knew he had been against the idea of breaking and entering the accountant's office, but hadn't realized how much the rest had bothered him.

"Angry? I'm livid. At this moment in time, they've gained everything they wanted and we have nothing except a possible breaking and entering charge to come, and a very rich guy's financial records."

"It's just information. And we've got a copy as well," I reminded him as we began the long walk back to the car.

My whole body ached, and I wasn't in the mood for yet another argument with Ben. There wasn't much more I could do but try to get the information Anthony had been trying to get. Especially as the only documentation he'd left us was so well encoded that we could barely glean enough clues from it to guess what he might have been doing.

An anger grew in me that matched the anger Ben was feeling about what we'd done. If Anthony had left better instructions and not been so cryptic, or told me what I was before he'd died, I wouldn't have been in this situation.

"It's not just information. It's the financial records of someone important. They're not just going to get a random person's financial information, Scarlet," Ben pointed out, finally sounding a little calmer.

"I know. But we've got a copy. We can check it out ourselves. We can see what they might have been looking for. Maybe even go and see this guy."

"That last part would definitely be a bad idea, but the rest is worth a try." Ben stopped walking as he spoke and motioned for me to hand my phone over.

"You want to look at it now?" I demanded.

"We should. Because if we want to do anything else

with it before we head to the city, we'll need to do it sooner rather than later. Right now, no one in the city knows we're anywhere but the center of LA."

It was a good point. After unlocking my phone, I handed it over and then looked expectantly at Ben to begin browsing it with me.

We stood in the shallows as the waves broke over our feet, and we looked at the photos. It was mostly bank statements from a particular period of time. It looked like this man had several income sources, and his funds were often invested into more tradable assets.

We scanned through it all for what felt like an age, not sure if anything was of any significance. While we did, the tide went out and the water receded until waves were no longer breaking over our ankles, but merely wetting our feet as they came rushing up the wet sand.

By the time we reached the last picture, our feet were standing on drying sand, having sunk slightly at some point. My neck also hurt from staying in the same angle, and we'd drained the battery on my phone halfway.

"I don't understand," Ben protested as I went back to the beginning.

"There's something here, or they wouldn't want it." I was about to tell him that I had payments of a similar amount as stated here.

"I know, but what if it's something we can't understand because we don't know what we're looking for?"

His thought bothered me and made me stop in my tracks. I didn't like unsolved mysteries at the best of times. This one was particularly infuriating.

For a moment, neither of us spoke, but Ben looked

around as if he'd just noticed that we were standing pretty much in the middle of the beach.

"Are the shadow catchers still nearby?" he asked.

"No. Not as far as I can tell." I was grateful for that much. It was now very late in the night, and I was getting tired. A part of me wanted to suggest that we should sleep and think about it when we were fresh and awake.

There was something about this mystery, however. It was begging to be solved now, and I was going to have to get a lot more exhausted before I'd be able to sleep.

Since we were safe enough, we agreed that it was silly to keep standing where we were. Neither of us wanted to stay on our feet, especially when we were already cold and tired.

Ben led the way back up the beach until we found a section of rock near the edge of the cliffs. It wasn't the greatest place to rest, and our legs still had to support us a little while we perched, but it was better than nothing.

Once more, we looked through all the data, trying to make heads or tails of what might be going on as well as the fund. It looked as if the guy was servicing too many debts. He was having money debited out for several loans and to several banks. But on top of that, he was making transfers to this strange fund. I drew Ben's attention back to it.

"The biggest payment from this account appears to be a standing order on a regular day of the month, and there's something about it that is sticking out to me," Ben agreed. "It's as if he was providing for something."

"Like a grant or maintenance payment to a kid, or trust

fund or whatever it is?" I asked, hoping he'd see what I had suspected.

"Yes, except this direct debit was part of his pension." Ben pointed out the transaction for the same amount each month.

It was as Ben pointed to it that I noticed the reference number for the standing order and realized it looked familiar, and I told Ben as much.

When Ben flipped to the next page I stopped him. I snatched my phone back, my mouth hanging open as my brain tried to catch up. It was all true. Not just a coincidence. Ben let out a dissatisfied noise about me interrupting but I couldn't have cared less about it right then. I had information to find to back up what I'd just discovered.

I logged into my own banking app and scrolled through the transactions. I'd been living in Detaris for the last little while and hadn't been spending any money. But the fund payments I had been getting were still there and easy to show, alongside the rent for the apartment that the same fund was also paying. And the reference numbers matched.

Several times over the past few years I had been surprised that the money kept coming, but I wasn't going to complain about it. I got to live and someone helped—I considered myself lucky. But the evidence was now staring me in the face.

"They're looking for *me*. Looking to see why there's someone giving me large sums of money. Trying to work out if I'm someone important. If I might be someone who can help them. If I'm the dragon heir."

"Only they don't realize that you're the recipient of the account this guy is setting up." Ben gulped.

"No, I guess not. If Jace knew, I think she'd have said." I exhaled as I glimpsed the ramifications of the knowledge I'd uncovered.

"But you can't be the heir. They just think you might be," Ben added. "Assuming that they're definitely looking for an heir. There's a chance that this could all be a big coincidence and they're looking into this guy because of someone else. If this guy knows about you, maybe he knows about other red dragons."

Although I hated to admit it, Ben had a point. There was a chance that I was just one of many red dragons being helped from that savings and investment account. Something about that thought didn't sit that well with me, however. I knew it was a sort of arrogance to want to be special, but being the heir—well, that gave life a whole new meaning.

"One thing we can agree on. It looks like they're looking for the red dragon heir. They've decided to try to tap us for information on a possible red guarded within city walls, or some such thing. One not out there where they can find him or her."

I wasn't sure I agreed with Ben, though I saw the point he was trying to make, but as far as I knew, I was the only red in the city.

There was an easy way to find out. "Why don't we ask them? It is bound to be easier on our bodies and definitely easier on my mind to know that we're trying to be honest and that we're being straight with them. I think it makes it more likely that we'll get respect and have them be straight with us."

Ben tilted his head to one side and looked at the financial page open in front of him one last time as the phone dimmed completely and shut down. It held my bank account details, and showed the same reference numbers. Something there connected me to these people. Possibly even what Anthony had been looking for.

"Okay. We should try to contact Jace again and get an explanation. But we need to be very careful."

"We're always as careful as we can be." I almost laughed. It didn't seem to be doing us much good so far.

CHAPTER FIFTEEN

After putting a message in the cave again, and thankfully getting out of it this time without encountering more shadow catchers, we went back to our car. Ben drove us to LA and the small apartment I still had.

I looked around it, wondering how such a small place out in the middle of nowhere could make me feel so much safer than some of the other options. But it did.

"I'll sleep on the sofa," Ben offered as I sat on the edge of my bed. I let him go, knowing it was best to sleep, even though I was sure I would struggle to do so.

Could I really be the dragon heir? Ben kept denying it, and he was possibly right. It was the exact sort of arrogant thought the rest of the dragons in the city were accusing me of, but someone was looking for me, and Anthony had been protecting me for a reason.

If I wasn't special in some way, why was all this fuss being made of me? Did it even matter whether I was an heir? I could do things with my abilities and the natural dragon magic I had that other dragons didn't seem to know how to do. Was that what everyone was looking for without realizing?

I tossed and turned trying to stop thinking about it. I had thought I was at peace with my past and not knowing who my parents were, but it hadn't taken long for all of this to unravel everything after all. What was going on and who knew what?

By the time morning came around, I was a mess of tangled hair, headaches, confused thoughts, and dreams that had faded in and out of each other.

And sweaty PJs.

"You look how I feel," Ben commented as soon as he saw me, never one to sugarcoat anything.

"We need to talk to Jace."

"You and I both agree. I want to know why they're looking into the finances of a man who clearly has a good heart. And why the hell he is giving you so much money. Then I think we need to go talk to him. Don't you?"

I lifted my eyebrows. He hadn't liked the idea when I suggested it last night, but it was the one that made the most sense. We had his address. It was on the documents.

This man had been making sure I had enough money for my entire adult life. I could at least ask him why.

"Right. Let's make sure we have everything else out of here we may need. Anything of Anthony's we want, too, in case we never get to come back at all, and then I know a good place to eat lunch." I grinned at Ben and he nodded.

"You know, you may be a pain in the ass sometimes, but I can see why Anthony believed in you. No matter what happens, you get yourself back up and figure out a way forward. There are a lot of people who give up and declare their circumstances too difficult."

"Being alone and having to solve your own problems will do that for you," I explained.

He nodded and we got to work. There wasn't much of my own stuff to gather, but we went down to Anthony's apartment. Almost immediately, both of us teared up. It reminded us of him so much.

Most of the damage had been cleaned up, and we'd already removed some of his belongings, but there were still a lot of memories. I went over to the board game cabinet. It had been cobbled back together roughly, no doubt so that a new janitor could move in at some point. It reminded me of where Anthony had hidden the journal for me to find.

I still wondered what it was he'd been trying to tell me, but I was getting closer to the answers. Whatever was going on, I was starting to figure it out.

Looking over the board games, I pulled out my favorites and the ones I remembered him loving or being really good at. Any that made me think of him in a way that made me smile.

Ben helped me, both with the games and collecting other things that must have been Anthony's when Ben knew him more. Things like ornaments and books. We tucked them all safely in the back of the car along with my stuff and then got in.

Neither of us spoke as we sat in the car. I looked over the building. It felt as if I was walking away from my old life entirely now. It was gone and I was done, but I didn't know what I was walking into instead. I didn't know what my future held. There were still too many questions.

Ben spoke up. "Let me know when you're ready to go. No rush. I know we're meant to be doing other stuff and I know you want other answers. But this should take as long as it takes."

He reached over and squeezed my hand. It was a gesture I knew well, and it made me almost start crying again. Exhaling, I looked over at Anthony's apartment one last time.

"Let's go find out what he knew and thought was worth dying for. Let's go make his death mean something." I tried to keep my voice even as I spoke, but didn't quite succeed.

"That's the perfect plan. I'm with you all the way." Ben pulled out, not needing any more encouragement.

It was a strange drive to the restaurant where we'd first met Jace and her colleague, and I was a little worried that we'd get a similarly annoyed welcome from the staff. I'd got the impression that they saw us as a nuisance.

Of course, there was a big possibility that I was a lot more than a nuisance. And I didn't know exactly what to think of Jace and her friends still. Ben disliked them as much as they disliked him, but he was willing to hear them out. It was something I appreciated.

As we pulled into the parking lot, I recognized several cars. No doubt some of them belonged to the staff. I'd just gotten out of Ben's car when a familiar face got out of a sedan nearby.

"Forgive my waiting for you like this." He came closer, leaning on his cane. Fintar. Another mystery.

It amused me to see him leaning so heavily on the cane,

given that I'd seen him run without it, but I nodded politely and didn't draw attention to what had happened the last time. Shadow catchers weren't pleasant topics of conversation, and I was curious enough about this guy to want to see what he had to say for himself.

His mass of white hair was as unruly as the last time, and his business card was still in my jacket pocket. In all the chaos, I'd not thought to use it.

"Hello, Fintar. Are you looking for me?" I asked, noticing Ben tense up much as he had when meeting this guy for the first time.

"In a manner of speaking."

Ben folded his arms across his chest. "Either you are or you aren't, old man. We're tired, have been chased by shadow catchers a lot lately, and we want answers from some people who really owe us now."

"That, I can understand. I might even be able to help. Forgive me if I seem to want something from you. I don't. Nothing that the world doesn't need as a whole. I place no extra burden upon you except to ask for a few minutes of your time."

"For some reason, I attract trouble if I stay in one place too long," I informed him. "You might not want to take more than a few minutes."

"That doesn't surprise me, and I think the reason why this keeps happening is beginning to dawn on you." He met my eyes and my blood ran cold. Did he know something about my bloodline?

Even Ben was too shocked to move. His mouth opened slightly.

"You've been digging up information for the new friends you've made, haven't you?"

"Maybe, maybe not. Now what do you need from me?"

He tilted his head to the side, seeming to study me. Beginning to think this was wasting our precious monster-free time, I also crossed my arms and tensed up. I was not okay being messed around with anymore.

"Forgive me. It's just almost hard to believe, but I think we all know it's true even though it shouldn't be possible. You believe it in your heart. That you're the heir. Don't you? You're not sure that you want to be. There's something in you that Anthony nurtured that wants to fight such an arrogant notion. But it is what you've started to believe, isn't it?"

I gaped, and even Ben no longer looked composed.

"How do you know?"

"Shadow catchers at every turn. So many dragons watching your every move. Money from unexplained sources. And power the average dragon doesn't even dare to dream of having, even if you can barely use it yet." He grinned as he listed what he obviously considered made me special.

It was clear he thought it was enough and was amused by our reactions.

"No one is going to want to believe I'm an heir. For one, apparently I'm too young."

"Are you? Do you know exactly when you were born?"

"I've got a birth certificate," I replied without missing a beat.

"And I've got two in my pocket that say I'm twenty-three or forty-one, but neither of them tell the truth of the hundred and six years I've seen as a dragon on this planet. We all know they can be forged, and I look older than both pieces of paper would suggest."

"That's conspiracy theory kind of talk." Ben set his jaw. "You're not helping us."

"I'm telling you that I believe that Scarlet here is the heir to the dragon throne and you're both confirming that you believe it too. Or would, if you weren't trying to find reasons it couldn't be true. But it is true. Everyone in the dragon city is going to try to find every little reason you're not, however. They don't want another heir. It's not good for them politically."

"I don't know if I want to be an heir," I shot back, still not sure I liked this conversation.

He chuckled.

"You need to find proof. And I know you're close. Find the proof and allies will come to your side. Talk to Jace about why an heir is important. Get all the information you can. You just need to go a little further and have her help, and I know you can put all the pieces together and prove your bloodline."

There was a screech of tires in the distance and this seemed to spook Fintar. He looked up and toward it as if he had been caught in the middle of some kind of heist.

"I think our time is up. Good luck, Scarlet. I know you'll make Anthony proud of you."

He turned and hobbled back to his car.

I watched him go, trying to process what he'd said.

"We should go inside," Ben whispered and gently took my arm to steer me that way. "Whatever else that guy might be right about, he knows we attract trouble, and I'm a little tired of trouble."

I had no argument with the sentiment so I let myself be encouraged inside. On top of that, I was hungry, and I'd begun to not only get used to the strange order needed to summon Jace, but I actually craved it.

It wasn't a combination I'd have ever tried if I hadn't been forced to order it, but there was something about potato and chocolate that just worked.

Ben didn't even have to tell the waiter where we wanted to sit. The moment he saw us, he waved us over to the booth and asked us if we wanted the usual order.

"Definitely. And we'd appreciate it to be as swift a service as possible. Things are a little more...urgent than normal. It's better for everyone if we don't linger in one place for too long."

The waiter raised his eyebrows at my words, but he jotted down our usual order, despite us having only ordered it twice. It made me wonder how many others showed up and ordered the same thing.

Or did every contact that came in here have their own special strange order? Having exactly the same one would make it suspicious to the chefs if they weren't in on it. Ours wasn't exactly a normal one.

Although I considered asking the waiter, he wasn't one for hanging around or making polite conversation. He wanted to just get on with what he needed to do and tend to the real patrons.

This time, however, I noticed that he didn't seem to be quite so calm. He glanced over at us frequently and his hands appeared to be shaking when he tried to put down our food.

"Are you doing okay?" I asked, trying to sound casual and as if I was asking a friend how their week had been when he came to check we were enjoying our meals.

"All as breezy as normal. Anything else I can get you both?"

I shook my head. I didn't believe him, but I didn't want to push. Something had him spooked and I couldn't figure out what. Ben frowned almost imperceptibly. He had picked up on it as well.

Given where we were and the point of our visit, I didn't feel as if I could ask him what he thought and begin a discussion on that subject, however. Who knew when we might be interrupted or if we'd be overheard? This was enemy territory, and we had to be careful while we were in it.

It was only as I ate another chocolate syrup–coated french fry that I wondered if there was something wrong with the food this time. What if they poisoned us or drugged us for being a nuisance. I stopped with the fries most of the way to my mouth and stared at it.

Ben followed my gaze as he lowered the food again. He lifted an eyebrow and then shook his head as if that settled the matter before taking one and eating it himself.

Before I could consider how to ask him if he was sure that we were okay, a guy I didn't recognize came over to our table. He was older and more rotund, and sounded a little out of breath, but comfortable being so. Behind him, I noticed Jace.

"It seems that we need to talk." He didn't sound pleased about it.

Although I had no idea who it was I was talking to, Ben's mouth fell open and his hand paused halfway toward claiming another french fry. I got the feeling that this was a dragon I should have known about. But I was entirely clueless.

CHAPTER SIXTEEN

There was an awkward silence as Ben moved over so our new contact could sit down, and I moved over for Jace. It continued once everyone was sitting, and I looked at each of my three companions, hoping someone would explain what was going on and why it was so tense in the entire restaurant all of a sudden.

Since our visitors had sat down, everyone in the building had been staring at our booth and the dragon opposite me.

Eventually, Ben broke the silence. "You're meant to be dead."

"Am I? I'll be sure to let my heart know it should stop beating to satisfy people's notion of reality when I'm done enjoying a good meal." The newcomer lifted his hand and summoned the waiter.

If I'd thought our server was shaking before, he was even worse now, but he carefully listened and wrote down the order. He went to leave right after, but our guest called him back.

"The lady hasn't ordered yet," he added motioning to Jace. The waiter gulped.

Jace looked as if she hadn't necessarily wanted food but now didn't feel as if she had a choice. After a brief pause, she asked for the carbonara, and I had to stifle a smile at her choosing one of the items we'd had to order to try to get an audience with one of them.

"Right, where were we?" he asked once our waiter had finally been allowed to leave again.

"You were apparently going to tell your heart to die, and then I was hoping that someone would explain to me why," I answered before anyone else could move a muscle.

The guy laughed and finally looked at me properly.

"You don't know who I am, do you?" he asked once he had calmed down.

I shook my head. "Am I supposed to know? Did you do something impressive?"

"Apparently, not dying when everyone thought I had, at least." He grinned and flicked me a wink.

"That would certainly get people talking, but I think there's at least two of us who can boast being alive when everyone would have considered us dead." It was a glib reference to it not being possible for me to be an heir and alive, but I wasn't sure he understood me. I had to move this on or I was going to lose this meeting before it properly began. "Let's start with the basics. Who are you and are you going to explain what I want to know?"

He sat back, acting like he was offended for about half a second.

"She really doesn't know anything," Ben added.

"Fair enough. Strikes me as funny for a red dragon.

Anyway, I'm Cios. I'm what you might call a steward. I guard the dragon throne for the next heir. Or I would, if I wasn't meant to be dead."

"So you are all looking for the heir?" I asked.

"Not exactly. Although to some degree, yes. I'm impressed that you got that from the information you picked up for us yesterday," Jace replied before Cios could.

"You want to claim the throne?"

"No. Not at all." Cios shook his head. "It might even be better if the throne remained empty. Monarchy isn't exactly in fashion anywhere in the world right now."

"Then what are your plans for the heir? This makes no sense at all." I frowned, confused, and I could tell that Ben wasn't faring much better. We had a lot of questions still.

"It's a long story. But we don't know how you fit into it. You seem to, in a lot of ways, but equally, you cannot. You're not old enough to be of the right lineage. Please don't get any delusions of grandeur. Yes, you're clearly a powerful red dragon and the shadow catchers are interested in you, but you aren't the heir, so I'm definitely not going to tell you things that are none of your business." Cios folded his arms across his chest.

I paused, not sure how to get them to give me the information I wanted. Were they right? Did I have delusional theories?

"You owe me information," I reminded them. "And this is what I want to know. I want whatever information Anthony was seeking. I've already given you the information you asked for in return for that. Everything else I want to know, which includes why you're meant to be dead and what you want an heir for if not the throne, I am trading for the extra information I have, information you don't even know you need yet."

There was a stunned silence as Cios looked at Jace and then back at me.

"You can put this one on me if you need to," Jace said to Cios. "Tell her everything."

Cios looked down and gathered his thoughts in an almost meditative fashion.

"There is a throne, yes, and if I were still under normal duty, my job would be to protect the rightful heir, my king or queen, and to ensure that no threat can be taken seriously. It is not an easy task, and I failed in the past. There have been dragon lords, and in at least one case, I could not get them to take the throne with the proper respect it deserved."

"Sounds like they didn't deserve the throne."

"No, not all those who would sit on one do. But I'm certain that a lesson in ethics is almost an entire waste of time given I am now a wanted criminal and you must be breaking several rules of the dragon city to be sitting across from me."

"Yes, that's a worthy point," I replied, though I didn't like to be thought of as being disobedient even when I was trying to follow the rules.

"The information you seek is all linked. The dragon on the throne is the dragon with the capacity to unite the dragon tribes and to also channel all the power from these dragons into holding the gate over the very depths of hell."

"Gate? Do you mean *the* gate? The thing that keeps some kind of massive demon from taking over the world?" No matter how many times I heard about his creature and the things it could do and how it was trapped, I felt as if I was missing some of the picture.

"Yes. It grows weaker over time. While the red dragon king trapped it a long time ago, contrary to what the elders tell the citizens in Detaris, it is not permanently trapped. The gate needs the dragon community to perform the ritual again, and for the red dragon in charge of our community to use our collective power to recharge it."

"Right, which is why you think I'm not the solution."

"You are not the solution. You are not the descendant."

"And your death?" I was not yet ready to argue or try to get the dragon to see a different point of view.

"An overseer or handler of the shadow catchers came after me once. With an army of the creatures. I got away, but every time I tried to do anything at all, he was there. Now that he thinks I'm dead and I operate in the shadows, I can at least do something to protect the throne and all it protects in turn."

I sat back and noticed that Ben's jaw was set and his fists were clenched. Cios looked at him, and the tension in the atmosphere grew rapidly.

"Of course, it's clear that you don't believe me. Why would I lie to you? You came and asked for information, and I have given it to you." Cios moved to get up, but I reached out a hand to get him to stay.

"Please, it's not that we don't believe. You clearly do, and it is obvious that you care about your role. We mean no disrespect to your conviction or passion to see the world safe." I tried to get the sincerity in my words across.

I watched Cios relax and settle again, and I felt better the moment he did.

"It's just that the elders in Detaris are very adamant that the gate is safe." Ben tried to explain, but it was clearly not going through properly. "And they say the shadow catcher activity lately is simply because someone is drawing them near with behavior they don't like."

Cios and Jace both laughed at Ben, and it drew the eyes of the other customers in the restaurant. They immediately fell silent.

"The elders don't want the world of dragons panicking because they've driven off their only hope of a savior. Who scared off the last red dragons in the city? How do they treat Scarlet?" Jace shot back.

I gulped, knowing the answer to one of those questions too well. Although I didn't want to put Ben on the spot or make him feel even more defensive than he already was, I looked at him for the answer to the first question.

"What happened to the other red dragons?" I asked when no one said anything.

"They fought between each other a lot. But the last two were driven out of the city, hunted and, according to the elders, killed." Ben wouldn't look at me.

"Killed? And you didn't think to tell me this before taking me to Detaris?" I heard the shrill inflection in my voice as I spoke, but I'd said it quietly enough that no one else appeared to notice.

"They were criminals, Scarlet. They weren't trying to be citizens."

"Criminals according to whom, Ben?" Jace asked. Her voice was even, and it cut through the atmosphere.

No one spoke in response.

"I have no reason to—"

I reached out and took Ben's hand, cutting him off.

"It's okay. It doesn't matter now. It's done, either way, and I'm in Detaris now. Also either way, we promised that we would find out what Anthony was trying to do, and I want to see that through."

Ben exhaled and visibly relaxed his shoulders and jaw. He gave my hand a squeeze again, but he didn't let go of me and I didn't let go of him. I took a deep breath, let myself study and be studied for a second, and then I turned back to our companions, who were waiting patiently for us to sort out our differences.

"Can you prove that the gate is weakening? And can you help me prove definitively that I either am or am not the heir?" I asked.

Cios nodded immediately at my first question, but both dragons looked at each other with wide eyes when I voiced the second.

"We really don't think you could be," Jace replied.

"I know, and everyone keeps saying that. But here's the information that I know that you don't. That guy whose information you wanted. It was for the trust fund he's created, wasn't it?"

Jace nodded, although Cios looked confused, as if he had no idea. He took Jace's word for it, though, and said nothing to stop me.

"Am I right in thinking that you believe he will lead you to the heir?"

"Possibly. He was working with someone to protect a dragon and has been for many years. He was one of the royal dragon guards and he was adamant until the end that the dragons driven from Detaris weren't criminals. Had he been in Detaris when that day came, it might have ended very differently."

"I am the beneficiary of the trust fund," I stated, trying to keep my voice calm despite the pounding of my heart in my chest. "I had no idea who was behind it or where it was from until I found you that information. My next task today was to go see the owner of that account."

Jace gulped, staring at me as Cios again looked between us.

"Can you prove it?" Her voice broke as her eyes watered up.

It felt as if it was a formality, her eyes telling me that she already believed me, but I nodded and pulled out my phone. I logged into my internet banking and searched for the reference that the fund payments were deposited with.

As soon as it was showing me the months and months of deposits, I turned my phone around and pushed it across the table. Neither Cios nor Jace touched it, but she pulled out print outs of the photos I had given her and laid them down beside my phone.

"How?" Cios asked.

"You believe?" Ben replied, more shocked than anything else.

"If you knew what we did about this fund and this dragon…" Cios let his voice trail off. "It makes sense. But you're too young."

"Yes… Everyone keeps saying that. But here I am, and where else has another red dragon come from? Who else could I be? I can combine our powers. Draw from all of us. Jace herself has more than enough proof of that." I felt a strange sense of calm grow inside me. I'd wondered who my parents might have been for so long, with no hope of finding the answers.

"She's our queen, Cios." Jace's eyes never left my face, her eyes wide with wonder.

I blinked, not expecting the weighty words, but it changed the atmosphere at the table entirely.

"No one is going to believe this." Ben squeezed my hand again. "But I'm beginning to feel like it doesn't matter if it's not true. You can save us. And if the gate really is weakening, then..."

"Let me show you. You both deserve to know more." Cios pushed my phone back to me but didn't let go, his eyes locking with mine. "Even if I am not sure. As your friend feels, I agree with his sentiment. You can save the dragon race. And there are no other red dragons that we know of. That makes you close enough to my queen that you have my protection and my service."

Not sure what to say, I looked at the three of my companions, and slowly all of them reached out, adding their hands where Ben held mine until all four of us were joined.

We stayed like that for several minutes, no one talking and nobody hiding the intensity of our emotion. Was I really likely to be the heir to the throne? I'd said it because it made the most sense to me at the time. But that was before I considered what that meant for me and living my everyday life.

In the same breath as being told I was a queen I had also been told that my parents had been chased out of the city I now lived in. And that they had been killed by this act. Of course, my mother at least must have survived a little longer, or I wouldn't be here. It was a huge revelation. To finally learn about my parents and that they had been in the city I was in now.

But something about it all didn't add up. I got the impression that no one had been able to rock the boat and demand answers in the past, so they might just not have any.

"I need proof," I insisted when none of us moved. I still had no idea if I wanted to be an heir, but either way I wanted to know for sure. "And I need it as soon as possible. Am I the heir to a throne or someone very similar to what you're looking for?"

Cios and Jace both nodded and got up, ushering me and Ben out as well. No one grabbed the bill to settle it, but no one chased us for payment, the staff even saying goodbye as if it had been settled already. I didn't know how, and it didn't matter at this point. I was starting to think the whole restaurant was in on whatever group these two worked for.

We were soon out of the door and ushered back to the car, and Ben was encouraged to follow Cios and Jace.

"Are you okay with this?" Ben asked me as he started the engine. "Wherever they're leading us, it could be dangerous."

"Everywhere I go seems to be dangerous. Anthony knew I was going to wind up in trouble at some point, and there are always shadow catchers if I stay anywhere too long. Even the city holds dangers for me. I have escorts to and from classes, and that's without anyone knowing I might be royalty. If I didn't want to face danger, I'm not sure I'd even have a choice at this point but to lie down and just die."

"You make a good point." Ben exhaled and gave a slight shake of his head. "A scary, sobering point, but a good point nonetheless."

"One of the things we used to say in the homes was that birth was like a lottery. Some people won it, some lost, and most people ended up somewhere in the middle. Some of us thought we'd lost. But we all knew that there were worse situations and that others weren't winning as much as it might appear. None of us would have wanted to be in this situation, however. To possibly be the last surviving heir to a royal line everyone but a few wants dead. Don't think I want to be an heir. Don't think that being royalty would be cool. I don't really want this. But these people are also telling me that Anthony died to keep me alive because I'm needed. Because if I don't survive, neither does the dragon race."

Ben glanced over at me and let out another breath.

"We might need some more help."

"We need proof I'm needed alive."

CHAPTER SEVENTEEN

After telling Ben how I felt and making it clear that I didn't wish for any of this to be true, we drove in silence. My life had changed so dramatically in such a short space of time that I really did just wish I was back in my old life, breezing easily from work to board games with Anthony. Life had been so much less stressful.

And it had been safe. There was a part of me that had forgotten what safe felt like.

We followed Cios and Jace for several hours as they drove east and away from the coast, LA, and the dragon city. I didn't know where they were going, but Ben didn't seem to be very surprised. It was safe enough in our cars, however, and I felt as if I could relax a little, especially with the troubles of LA and the other dragons behind us.

Eventually we reached a dirt area off the side of the road, in among the trees, where people could park and go into the forest to camp or take a daytime stroll. A few cars were scattered about in the parking area, but it was a quiet afternoon and late enough that no one with any sense was going to start walking now.

"This is going to take another hour or so to get to at least," Jace said and pulled out a couple of big bottles of water and large packets of trail mix.

Ben took the offered items and shoved them in a rucksack he kept in the trunk of the car. I thanked all of them before we set off, Cios going ahead, then Ben, me, and finally Jace.

A part of me tensed up and my stomach threatened to empty as I followed these people I hardly knew into the trees. Not only had awful things happened the last time I had been in a forest, but I didn't know either of these dragons at all. My trust was at an all-time low.

I'd only been walking a few minutes when I realized that I could also feel something ahead. A presence. It was like the shadow catchers in that it was uncomfortable and foreboding—but not one of them.

I stopped, closing my eyes and concentrating on it.

"Scarlet, are you okay?" Ben reached out for my arm.

"She can feel it. Where we're going," Cios replied. "Can't you? I imagine you can feel the shadow catchers too."

"Yes," I replied, grateful that he knew about my capabilities. It decreased the odds that he was luring me into a trap. If he knew that I was going to feel my enemies coming, then he knew it would mean I could just run away from it.

It still made me wary, however, and I stayed where I was, feeling the entity with my mind and trying to work out exactly what it was.

"It's the gate, isn't it?" Ben added. "You're leading us to the gate. Or whatever part of it stands in the mortal realm."

"Yes. Not all the way there. I have a feeling that Scarlet won't need to get close to feel the truth in our words."

"I need more proof than just what I will be able to feel. If this is to work and I am to help, then I will also need to prove to others that there is need of a red dragon."

Cios frowned and tilted his head to the side as if he was thinking.

"I can get you evidence of a sort. Whether the elders of Detaris will believe it for what it is or remember the way something used to be is not something I can say, but it is all the proof that exists."

"Then we shall all have to hope that it's enough," I replied.

We moved off again, heading down the trail and toward the uneasy feeling in my head. The closer I got, the heavier the feeling grew and the more tired my body felt.

I noticed it in the others too. Everyone appeared weary far sooner than we ought to have, and all of us were struggling along before we'd been walking for more than twenty minutes.

Something oppressive was in the area ahead. Knowing what the dragons had trapped beyond the gate, I was starting to get an idea of why this was out in the middle of nowhere.

Over the next five minutes, the path also shrunk, grew less trodden and more overgrown, until Cios raised a hand and began to use some kind of magical power to gently encourage the plants to shy back from the path and grow in a new direction.

I was grateful for the extra relief. The heavy feeling to my feet was hard enough to combat as it was. This was the strangest, most difficult walk I had ever been on, and I couldn't entirely pinpoint why. My soul felt heavy, my body weary. And it shouldn't have.

Cios moved slower now, more cautiously, but both Ben and Jace struggled to keep up.

To help me keep going, I counted the steps I was making in my head, focusing on increasing that number and internally praising myself for getting it higher and higher. It was the sort of strategy I used whenever I had to do anything difficult. Focus on just the task and the numbers running through your head.

It helped block out pain and discomfort and kept my body in a rhythm that made it easier. And it kept me from focusing on the increasingly uneasy feeling from the threat ahead.

Eventually, I had to stop, my mind swimming under the constant weight.

"What's behind that gate?" I asked as I noticed how much pain I was in just from standing there.

"A demon. Well, *the* demon, to be very precise." Cios paused again and turned.

Ben was offering me food and drink. I wasn't sure I could keep the snacks down, but I accepted the bottle and sipped the water.

"If you're thinking in human terms, you might even call this thing Satan. It's the biggest evil the world knows. There's a massive gate holding him at bay, but he's on the other side and trying to get back into this world. And even with the gate there, his power isn't entirely contained."

"Which is why there's shadow catchers," I replied, knowing some of this from the lessons in the dragon city. Of course, they'd not gone into quite this much detail, but they'd come close.

"Unfortunately he can't be contained entirely. He can exert his will here in ways the dragons have never been able to stop. You'll see more as we get closer."

"I'm not sure I can get closer." I panted and sipped more water.

"We can't feel what you're feeling, but my guess is that you can dull your senses to it as well," Cios said. "You've been trying to sense the shadow catchers so you're aware of danger as soon as possible, and that makes you more attuned to feeling it than not."

"Pretty much. You would too if they showed up anytime you were outside for more than five minutes." I straightened up and focused on blocking out some of the feeling of dread. If I dulled the presence of this demon, how could I be sure I wasn't going to make it harder to notice his minions? Not that it mattered much, but I got the impression he wanted nothing more than to see me dead.

That thought alone made me hesitant to move forward at all.

"Is this safe in any way?" I asked as I handed my water bottle back to Ben. "Taking the only surviving red dragon you know of toward the devil?"

Cios grinned for a fraction of a second before looking more serious again.

"We believe so. And you are not alone out here. I also

understand that you know how to hurt shadow catchers by channeling the powers around you."

It was my turn to nod.

"Then by virtue of you being here with three other dragons, as long as we and you have strength left in our bodies, you are safe."

I opened my mouth to make some kind of retort about that not being much of an assurance, but it was such a surprising statement of faith in me being the one who would keep us all safe that I didn't know how to respond.

"Just focus on shutting it out. On keeping the feeling of the enemy at bay, behind a glass wall or locked in a cabinet," Cios offered.

This was possibly one of the stupidest things I thought I'd ever heard, but I didn't have anything to lose by giving it a try, so I did as he suggested.

Taking several deep breaths, I closed my eyes again and tried to isolate the feeling of dread in my mind, and then I imagined putting it in a glass-fronted box and pushing it away.

As I did the last part, I opened my eyes and looked up. For now, I felt a little better. With no idea how long it would last, I decided to move forward while I could.

"I really hope we don't have much further to go." I shook my head at the mental strain this was putting me under on top of everything else.

Ben slipped his hand into mine again and gave me a familiar look. If nothing else, I wasn't alone. He might not have believed that I was the heir, but at least he was going to help me as much as he could.

"Can none of you feel it?" I asked as we continued. My

mind wanted something else to focus on other than the counting of numbers and the placing of one foot after the other like a mechanical robot.

"Nope. Not yet."

"We can feel you, however," a voice said as someone stepped out of the shadows of the trees and into the path ahead of us.

We all stopped as I locked eyes with the tall man. His face was stern, and his muscular body was clad in dark greens. His skin was dark enough that he looked as if he could blend in with the forest itself.

"Good evening." I hoped he was going to explain his angry sounding tone without me having to ask him about it.

"No one goes beyond this point. I'm going to have to ask all four of you to return the way you've come."

"We can't, Merrik," Cios insisted. "She needs to see the gate and what it does to the world around it now."

"I'm under orders to not let anyone through, especially someone who isn't one of our allies." Merrik shook his head and lifted one of the same shields I'd seen the black dragons in Detaris use to defend themselves.

Cios went to carry on or argue, but I put my hand out, reaching the taller dragon's shoulder and stopping him.

"It's okay." I turned back to Merrik. "I know you are trying to do what you believe is right. You are protecting this area and trying to keep all dragons safe like any black dragon would do, aren't you?"

"We all have a role to play, ma'am."

I nodded and lifted my hand.

"That we do. And I know mine. I simply ask that you

respect mine as I do yours." As I spoke, I morphed my hand into a claw as I had done in the past to climb trees with no branches. But most importantly, to show the color of my scales.

His eyes went wide and then he looked at the others and me as if he wasn't quite believing what he was seeing.

"We need to get through. She needs to see the gate," Cios repeated, putting his hand on Merrik's shoulder. "And it's very important that no one knows what you just saw until we have proof of her heritage and she's ready to make the claim open to her."

"Are you sure? They will want to know. I will have to give them something."

"Would I be standing here protecting her and guiding her if I wasn't? Do you think I'd truly make this walk if something hadn't convinced me of the truth?"

The conviction in the dragon's words sent a shudder up my spine that I tried to suppress. I didn't want this—not knowing what I was going to have to do—but it seemed I didn't have much choice now but to attempt it. And that thought was terrifying.

Merrik eventually backed up and let us through, but I saw the fear in his eyes and the way he gripped his shield. Despite seeing that I was a red dragon, he wasn't convinced he was doing the right thing in letting us through to the gate, and I wasn't sure that I blamed him.

We carried on, the pressure of what lay ahead giving me a headache but making me even more determined to try to find a way to get proof that the gate had weakened. To some degree, I was relying on Ben to know what that would look like, but Cios and Jace also appeared to believe they could tell me what I needed to know.

Another mile passed under our feet, and the pain in my head and body increased further.

"I think I'm beginning to feel something," Ben said, his voice barely above a whisper as he squeezed my hand.

I returned the gesture but carried onward.

"We all feel it now, and you're about to see why," Cios told us. I was already suspecting the gate wasn't far. The trees were starting to look different and feel different, and there was a strange smell in the air.

When we'd walked another few yards, I saw through the tree trunks and foliage that there was a clearing of sorts beyond. After a few more steps, I realized it wasn't a clearing at all. It was a dead zone. All the trees and bushes, all the wildlife in this section were dying. And everything beyond it was already dead.

We took a few more steps until we were spread out along the tree line. Every tree trunk was blackened and warped. In front of us lay a few yards of growing mold, a white fungus that stank, and beyond that was nothing but a pile of black slime and stench.

Cios reached out a hand, and I saw a patch near us recover enough that I could have stepped out onto it if I'd wanted to. It appeared to tax him enormously to encourage it to grow.

Ben pulled out his phone and started recording a video. I watched as Cios stopped trying to make the small patch better. It was as if the same power was being operated in reverse, slowly eating away at everything healthy until it was back to the blackened state it had been in when we arrived.

"The gate is over a mile that way," Cios said as Ben lifted the camera to show everything that lay beyond. The view showed the forest in the far background and the large two mile wide circle around the gate, all of it decayed and decaying.

"The stories of the red dragons sealing the gate always mention a path right up to it." Ben spoke loudly enough that it would be picked up by the phone.

"Yes. And if a red dragon brought us all here and combined our powers, they could push back the evil and resecure the gate, but without a red dragon, there's nothing we can do."

"Any red dragon?" Ben asked, but again, we were all pretty sure of the answer.

"The heir."

I stepped forward, reaching for everyone to take my hand and let me use their power, not sure what I was going to prove. I wanted to try and show them I was different and might be the heir they were in need of, but there was a commotion behind us. Ben shut his phone off and stuffed it into his pocket before I could do anything else.

I panicked, thinking it might be shadow catchers, but dragons appeared, most of them in human form. Merrik was with them. It seemed our excursion was over.

CHAPTER EIGHTEEN

The leader of this new group of dragons insisted that we were trespassing and needed to leave, and then a tense silence fell over us all.

"Delphin, don't be like this. You know that—" Cios tried once more to stand up for us before I interrupted him with another touch of my hand.

"It's okay. We have enough. I should go before danger finds all of us."

"You should listen to the girl and get out of here. Merrik told us what you tried to claim. And we all know she's too young." Delphin glared at all of us.

I frowned, not liking his tone but taking the hint. Everyone thought I was too young, and I was going to have an uphill battle proving that I was an heir. If I even was one. Either way, I wasn't going to achieve anything here, and the constant pain and pressure was beginning to make me feel sick as well as hurt.

Before anyone else could bother arguing or make the situation any worse, I turned to walk away from the strange, decayed area of the earth and the pressure in my head.

Until next time, a voice said, making me turn around to see who'd had said it, but no one was even looking at me. Ben raised his eyebrows as if he had no idea what I was doing.

"Did you hear that?" I whispered to him as I gave his hand another squeeze.

He shook his head, the puzzled look on his face growing even deeper. His eyes searched me for an explanation, but I wasn't going to give one right now. I suppressed all the emotions I wanted to show.

Part of me that knew I'd just heard the voice of whatever lay on the other side of the gate. And if he'd spoken to me and not to anyone else, it was yet another sign that he saw me as a worthy opponent. From what I'd been told, no one could oppose the power of the demon behind the gate but the true heir.

But now I needed to prove that to at least the elders in the dragon city so I could gather the dragons to reinforce the gate and learn how to do it.

The trek back to the cars had me on edge the whole way. My mind still felt the presence behind the gate so strongly that I feared I wouldn't be able to feel any shadow catchers in the area.

When we were about two-thirds of the way back, we stopped to drink some water. The others snacked, although I refused food once again. It was then that I felt the shadow catchers in my mind, likely only because I was preoccupied by the fear that I'd miss the telltale signs.

Immediately I froze, spilling some water down my chin,

my eyes going wide as I became aware that we were not alone.

"Shadow catchers," I whispered as Ben took the bottle of water and stuck the lid back on.

"How many and where?" he asked as Cios ushered me forward again.

"I can't say exactly, but on at least three sides. We need to run."

My companions didn't need to be told twice, and we all started to sprint. Despite our need to hurry, they formed up in a triangle around me, Cios leading with Ben and Jace behind me and to either side.

I wasn't sure what they thought they could do to protect me that I couldn't do for myself, but it was nice to know they cared enough to want to try.

The shadow catchers moved faster than any I'd ever felt before, rushing through the forest toward us, but I had enough warning that we still had some level of safety.

It wasn't long before I heard others sprinting behind, the sound of several booted feet on the hard dirt and limbs rushing through leaves and branches with no thought for personal safety.

I glanced back to see Merrik and another person, both of them carrying shields and strange-looking spears.

The sight would appear terrifying to the casual observer, but their company filled me with hope. If I had been able to repel and harm shadow catchers by drawing on the power of other dragons, having two more with me was an asset.

"Something has drawn the wrath of the dark one," Merrik reported. "Is it this dragon?"

"Yes. Because they know I'm powerful and important even if you don't," I replied, shocking even myself. I heard Cios chuckle. "But you can stop worrying. You're actually safe with me if you let me connect with you too."

This made them pause, but I wasn't going to wait any longer to let his thoughts catch up. I'd already wasted enough time, and the shadow catchers behind us had been given several seconds to catch up to us.

With a nod to my companions, I set off running again and hoped they would all get the message and come with me. I still couldn't quite believe what I'd dared to say, but I was being hunted by shadow catchers, I was surer than ever that I was the heir to the dragon throne, and the most powerful evil in the world had gotten into my head. I didn't have time for people who couldn't get past prejudice, fear, or tradition.

For a few minutes all I heard was the six of us racing through the forest undergrowth and pounding on packed dirt, tree roots, and grass. Eventually there was another sound: shadow catchers slithering through bushes and sucking the moisture from them as they passed, leaving only decayed husks behind.

We weren't far from the vehicles now, but the shadow catchers were going to catch up to us first.

When the first shadow catcher came within ten yards of us and we still couldn't even see the cars yet, I had to act.

"Shield and spear," I yelled as I spun to face the creature. "And everyone put a hand on my shoulders and get behind me."

At first, Merrik and his friend didn't move, but as Ben, Jace, and Cios did as they were told without question and the shadow catcher came closer, Merrik spun his shield around so I could grab the strap inside.

I snatched the spear too. Bringing the spear and shield together, I pulled on all the energy and power I had, as well as that of the dragons connected to me. Both the two new dragons hesitated to touch me and join in, but I felt a boost to the power and a difference to it that I hadn't felt before.

I saw their eyes go wide as everyone shuffled behind me, trying to squeeze themselves into a tiny space one person wide. There was very little time to charge the items I wore the way I imagined, but I did my best and held firm as the shadow catcher ran at me.

It impaled its body on the spear and smacked into the shield with enough force to knock me back. There was a deafening screech, and the creature went limp.

"You've killed it," Merrik said in shock.

"I'm not sure I have." I was still able to feel a strange dark presence from it, but it wasn't moving and seemed to be stuck on the end of the spear.

As I stopped channeling power to the weapon and shield, the tip of the spear began to decay, as anything did when it came into contact with the shadow catchers.

"Sorry," I offered as I pulled it out and looked at the guy I'd snatched it from.

"I think you'd better keep it. And I owe you an apology."

"We can work that out somewhere else." I felt more of the monsters bearing down on us, although they had paused after hearing the pained screeches of the frontrunner.

My entire group turned again and headed for the cars. My steps were slowed by the weight of the shield and the unwieldy nature of the spear that remained a burden as I tried to run along as fast as I had before.

I felt a little light-headed and as if I'd drained myself in some way I couldn't explain. There was so much stress and difficulty in my life, I didn't feel as if I could cope with anything else, like how this power combination worked and why it felt as if I was both powerful and weak every time I did something like this.

At the back of my mind, I had the constant feeling and threat of all the evil in the area as well. Whatever was hidden behind the gate was a powerful presence, and all the smaller ones were still converging on me. It made me feel on edge, like there was a constant irritating noise in my head that was loud enough to be noticed when everything was quiet but not near enough to do anything about.

It made everything a little bit harder.

Finally the clearing with the cars and the dirt parking lot could be seen up ahead. A bunch of people with a light and several flashlights appeared to be in a huddle in the middle of the area, having a discussion and poring over a map.

"You might want to get in your cars and leave," Ben warned as he reached the clearing. Cios joined him in encouraging them away, while Jace ran to the car to get it unlocked and pull open the driver's door.

It was strange to hear the dragons I was with being less subtle about the dangers of the shadow catchers. I was sure they'd left humans to take their chances in the past, but things had clearly changed. Perhaps it was the close encounter we'd just had, or maybe they'd found their moral compass now that they were near the heir meant to save them all. As for me, I simply wanted to keep everyone safe and cared less about them finding out about magic or that we existed.

But the people weren't particularly responsive, remaining in their huddle and now looking between us and their map. I moved to them, their eyes all going wide as they saw my shield and rotted spear.

"Please," I insisted. "You need to leave. There's something dangerous out there and it's coming this way."

"Like a bear?" one of them asked as Merrik went to another car and unlocked it.

"No, something a thousand times worse than a bear."

One of the humans scoffed, a man in his forties.

"Amusing tale. And I like the outfit to go with it, but we're here to take a look at something we spotted with our drones and enjoy the quiet of night. We're not easily scared off and—"

"You don't get it," I replied, my tone getting deeper and lower as I felt anger rise inside me. "I'm not making up some fanciful story. You're all in very real danger."

In the back of my mind, I felt two more shadow catchers getting closer, coming from different sides but all heading straight here as if they could sense me as much as I could sense them.

"Come on, Scarlet," Ben called, half in the driver's seat of our car while Cios and Jace were already getting in theirs.

"I'm not leaving these people to die," I yelled back. Some of the hikers were finally starting to get the idea that something really nasty was happening.

There was a pause as no one moved, but they all stared at me.

As a shadow catcher could be heard coming closer, Ben ran back to me. I was pretty sure that he intended to try to drag me away, but Cios and Merrik also hurried toward me.

This spurred on Jace and the other dragon to join me as well, and soon they were behind me again, all the humans being ushered behind us in a tight cluster. I lifted the shield and spear again as all five of my dragon companions reached out and touched me in some way.

"We're breaking so many rules," Ben whispered.

I ignored him and channeled all our energy again, feeling it come from their bodies and through mine. Once again, it sucked power from me as well and charged the shield and spear, hardening them and making them crackle with electricity. This time they also glowed a little, my mind growing better at balancing the power coming from each source.

The shadow catcher came toward me and everyone else, and the gasps, squeals and shouts from the humans behind me almost distracted me. I lunged forward, hoping my small dragon force would follow as I stabbed yet another demon and wounded or killed it.

It let out another loud screech, but I didn't leave the spear in its stomach this time. Pulling back, I looked for the second shadow catcher that had been approaching.

This one was hanging back, almost as if it was scared or at least wary of being killed. I didn't know how they communicated with each other or if it could learn something from seeing the other two shadow catchers fall, but I couldn't let it figure out a better way to attack us.

"Dragons, with me," I called, turning to face the shadowy creature.

At first, they didn't respond, and the humans seemed to be scared enough that they wanted to huddle after me too. I had made myself look like some sort of general in battle, and that meant I was likely to be the one everyone rallied behind. I was also the one wielding the shield and spear.

One part of my ensemble was looking worse for wear. The spear had held up better the second time as I had pulled it back out more swiftly. Still, it was now barely more than a pointed branch, and not something worthy of being called a weapon.

I had at least one more shadow catcher to contend with, which meant that I was going to have to make do. With the dragons around me finally reacting and the humans huddling even closer together behind me, I finally began to turn the group so we faced the dangerous creature head on. I felt the contact of five dragons again, all of them placing a hand on my shoulders or back.

Together, we moved forward, my pace slow so I wouldn't lose them, my eyes locked on the target and my mind already starting to connect to the magic in the others. It was a strange feeling to be able to control and use the power in the dragons around me, but it was already making me feel exhausted.

It seemed like this was going to be the last time I could pull this trick this evening, and it made me wonder how I was meant to have the strength to draw from an entire race, or at least city, of dragons to shore up the massive gate nearby. Just the thought made me want to sleep for a week.

Instead of giving in to the desire to rest, I moved forward, setting my jaw and looking for the opportunity to strike.

This shadow catcher danced to the side as I came close and missed my first jab with the spear. Its beak struck my shield with an almighty clang that jarred my arm and made me stagger back a step.

For a brief moment, the connection between me and the others was broken, but the power lingered in the shield and spear long enough that I could block a second screeching attack.

Once again the shield appeared to hurt the creature, but unlike the previous times I'd fought shadow catchers and won, this one didn't recoil as if it was too hurt to fight on. Instead, it yelled and prepared to come at me for a third time.

I funneled the power from my allies and adjusted my position just enough that the blind creature did the same as its two predecessors and impaled itself on the spear.

Again, I was stuck. The creature weighed a lot more than I'd have expected something that appeared to be a shadow to weigh. As the spear decayed even more and I tried to shake it down and forward, there were yells from behind me.

"There's more of them coming." Merrik pointed to the forest path we'd been running down.

"Really is time to go, then," I suggested as I turned again.

This time, the humans didn't need any encouragement

to leave, and I let Ben take my hand and tug me back to our waiting car. He had left the engine running and gunned it as soon as we were inside. Jace and Cios came with us, Cios having given the keys to his car to Merrik and the other guard. The group of humans got in the only other car present.

As a small convoy, we hurried onto the road, heading back in the direction of LA. We were all safe at last, and if nothing else, I had proof of two very important things. That the gate was weakening, and that I could do something no one expected a dragon to be able to do.

CHAPTER NINETEEN

For a while no one spoke while I sat in the back of the car, exhausted, shaking and still holding a shield and almost completely rotten spear. My mind kept playing the events of the last hour or so on a loop, the blackened, decaying land with the gate barely visible in the center of it and fighting shadow catchers in prime position.

And finally, the humans. The fear on their faces as they'd run for the safety of their vehicle made me very glad that I'd saved them, but I'd also broken yet another rule.

At least this time, I had the advantage of only having Ben with me. He would never say anything to anyone, even in the elders' chambers where it was impossible to lie. It would get him in as much trouble as me. He was my legal guardian, and I was officially part of his line of dragons, despite the color difference.

Cios looked back from the passenger seat at me. "You can relax now." He offered to take the spear and I handed it over to him. It was almost useless now anyway.

"I still need my proof that I'm the heir." I couldn't quite

relax yet. I was starting to handle myself better, but I wasn't all the way there, and if I was going to convince the city to stand with me and take on the evil behind the gate, then I needed to make it clear that I was who I said I was.

That was a very scary thought. But it was time.

Looking down at the shield on my lap, I decided that even though the hardness of the metal was compromised and no longer as solid, there was something about it that I wanted to hang onto. It wasn't quite like the shields in the city. It had been easier to charge.

"Do you know what is different about this shield?" I asked Ben when a few more minutes had passed and it was still bugging me.

"Different?" he asked, holding his hand out to feel it.

"Yeah. It is harder and a lot more responsive than the city ones."

As I spoke, he ran his hand along the surface of it. Unlike the shields we had back at the city, it hadn't decayed even one tiny bit. And that was after we had fought off three shadow catchers. It was a lot for one shield to tackle.

"I think the folks here know that certain elements and magic can be combined to make something that is part both."

I nodded. It made sense. They seemed to know a lot more about red dragons and what it might mean for what I was capable of, and they definitely knew more about the gate and its purpose and maintenance. From everything I had learned in the school, it appeared that the dragon elders were simply ignoring the gate and acting as if it would always do its job.

"If you still want proof that you're the red dragon heir,

then there might be one way we could get it," Jace ventured a few minutes later. I blinked a few times, surprised that she was offering it to me.

"Go see the guy paying the trust fund," Cios finished for her.

Given that it was one of the avenues Ben and I had been intending to try, I certainly had no objection to looking into it. But we had more people in tow now, both dragons and humans. It was a bit of a problem, and I wasn't entirely sure of the best way to fix it.

"Can we stop off somewhere dragon- and human-friendly where I can have a quick chat with those hikers we rescued?" I asked when we continued down the road.

"What about that café we stopped in that one time? Where we traded those lobsters for some dinner," Ben suggested.

"Are we near enough?"

He tilted his head to the side and then shook his head.

"I know somewhere not far from here," Jace offered. It was a safe enough bet, so I nodded and turned to make sure the other two cars were following us. I wanted to talk to all of them even if I wasn't sure exactly what I wanted to say to them yet.

Within ten minutes, Ben pulled into a late-night diner on the edge of a small town. It was lit up with neon lights that looked as if they could do with some maintenance. One section flashed on and off. The other two cars came into the parking lot after us and everyone got out.

"Are we safe now?" one of the human guys asked.

"I hope so. Will you let me buy you all something to eat

and answer your questions?" I offered as Merrik and his friend also came closer. "All of you."

I didn't get any arguments from any of them, so I led everyone inside. The waitress was slightly surprised that I wanted a table for ten but didn't seem to mind when we offered to push a couple of bigger tables together and set them back straight when we were done.

Cios and Merrik worked together to make it happen, while Ben and I got started on ordering us all some food and I pulled out one of my bank cards to pay for it and make sure they knew we were good for the money in advance.

One of the advantages of living in Detaris but still getting a trust fund paid monthly was that I would still have money coming in but wouldn't need to use it for very much. I could handle paying for this, especially as I needed to have everyone focusing on being reasonable for a while.

As soon as we'd ordered and had our drinks, I looked around at the group, trying to figure out where to begin.

"What were those things?" the hiker spokesperson asked.

"We call them shadow catchers," Merrik answered before I could. "Although you might call them demons."

"Demons exist?"

"Aye, and the devil as well." Cios frowned. "If any of you have any sense, you won't go and try to find that strange area of the land you saw. It's…not safe."

There was a silence as the humans looked between each other. I was pretty sure that they already knew that would be a bad idea.

"Do you protect that area, then?" one of the women asked.

"Some of us do," Merrik replied. "Some of us were just seeking answers and trying to learn more. We are trying to make sure no one comes to any harm. And we've kept that area safe for a long time. We need you to help us keep it safe by not telling anyone. Word always gets out, and then some people show up thinking that they're sent by God or whatever and they get themselves hurt or endanger others."

"We get it. Not sure anyone would really believe us anyway," the original guy said.

"I do have one more question, though," the woman added. "Are you some sort of magical race? What you did and the way you seemed to come together and combine your...powers. Was that some kind of Avengers or Power Rangers deal?"

"Something like that," I replied. "Not all of us can do it. We don't understand that entirely either. But it's the only way we've found to hurt shadow catchers. And it takes at least three of us, preferably more."

"What our very modest friend here means to say is that she might be the only...person alive who can do it, and it's to do with her genetics and bloodline, and until we know why, the more people involved just means the more she has to protect and the more we wear her out. So for her sake and ours, we really can't have any more people getting into trouble." Ben smiled as he spoke, clearly trying to satisfy their curiosity enough, but also make sure they backed off.

One of the women reached out to me and squeezed my hand across the table.

"You saved our lives when you clearly didn't have to. And if that came at a cost to you, then that was even more amazing than before. Thank you. We'll keep your secret. I hope you can figure this out. I'm only a biologist, and I study plants more than humans, but if there's anything that I can do to help and somehow repay the debt we owe you, then, please, tell me."

I squeezed her hand back, unable to speak for a moment. This wasn't what I had expected at all.

"Thank you. All of you. For understanding. I hope one day I can tell you all more and everyone is safe again."

"Don't we all," the first guy replied. "But one thing that I know from being on this planet as long as I have is that there's always some battle that some people are fighting somewhere for the good of something. I can save plants and help our world that way. You clearly have other gifts and have other fights to win. I'm not going to get in your way or make it harder."

I exhaled with relief, grateful that they were being so reasonable. It made it easier to trust that they'd keep our secret. At least for a while. I knew enough of human nature to know that one of them or several of them would say something at some point.

As soon as they'd eaten, the four of them excused themselves and returned to their car. I didn't move, sure I needed to say something to Merrik and his friend.

"Thank you, both of you, for standing with me this evening," I offered when it looked like they might get up and leave as well. "I don't know how I can do what I do, but I know that you made a difference, and I couldn't have done as much as I did without you."

"I've been guarding that site almost my whole life," the tall dragon said, giving me his full attention. "I'm Alitas."

Ben, Jace, and Cios all collectively gasped, and I looked at the three of them as they stared at him. I could only assume that his name meant something to them. Only Merrik didn't appear to be surprised by this.

"I'm sure that your name means something incredibly important, but I'm sorry, until about three weeks ago I didn't know I was even a dragon. There's clearly a lot lacking in my knowledge. Why does your name carry such great weight?"

"I'm the last captain of the royal guard. It was my job to protect the royal line and the gate and oversee the other royal guard. I am the person that failure rests on."

I blinked, surprised to have met someone so important and have used their spear the way I had.

"I'm sorry I broke your weapon. I hope it wasn't ceremonial."

Alitas threw his head back and roared with laughter. Again, I looked at my companions, not understanding what was so funny, but other than Merrik, who was smiling, they seemed as confused as I was.

Eventually he calmed down and then he waited for the waitress to stop staring at us, his sudden outburst loud enough that everyone had looked our way, even if only briefly.

"I have pledged to the royal red dragon line to use my spear to protect the red dragon line and the gate, and in all my years of service it never saw battle. Today I was given the honor of fulfilling my duty for the first time. When the line of red dragons fell and we thought you were all gone, the shame nearly killed me. All the years after the last king fell and other red dragons tried to take on the challenge, I watched them fall one by one, not one of them worthy enough. Yet you apologize to me? When you have given me not only my hope back, but my duty, my purpose, and my honor all in one action?"

"You think she is the heir, then?" Merrik asked while I was still reeling from his words.

"How can anyone not see it? I've never met or felt another red dragon who could so instinctively channel not only their own power but draw on and combine the magic of those nearby. It is a gift the royal bloodline held. Other red dragons could do so after much concentration, and the king even believed that there might be a way to teach all dragons to use their power in such a way, but if this young woman didn't even know that she was a dragon until recently, then she has certainly not been trained or taught."

"No, that's something I can very definitely claim," I replied. "I haven't been trained very much yet, and the school in Detaris can only teach me so much in such a short space of time."

"Which brings me to my next question. What will you do now, my queen?"

It was the second time someone had called me that in one day, and I wasn't sure I liked the sound of it. I was maybe the heir, and I could accept that notion reluctantly, but I sure as anything didn't want to rule over anyone. Just hearing it again made my mind freeze, until Ben reached over and squeezed my hand again.

"We need to find some proof either way of Scarlet's heritage," Ben answered for me.

"And I am probably going to have to learn an awful lot more. And train or something. If the gate is weakening, then at some point we are going to need to strengthen it, are we not?"

"Yes. And forgive me for being blunt, but you're not ready for that. It wasn't something the royal line had to do very often, and it took a lot of work to get ready." Alitas frowned as he spoke, and I felt the weight of his words.

It confirmed what I already feared—that my parents had left me a bigger legacy to fulfill than I'd ever wanted, and I was going to have to rise to the challenge or an entire world could die because of me. No pressure.

Alitas went on, "Then I will return to my post with Merrik, and we will await any communication we receive on how things progress. If you ever need me, my very being is yours to command."

"Thank you. For now, continue with the good work that you have done for so long and know that you have my respect for having continued to carry out your duties when you must have felt no hope and no point to doing so."

Alitas bowed toward me, Merrik following suit, and then the two of them left. Not sure what else to do and not wanting to speak to anyone else just yet, I made a beeline for the counter to pay for our meal, not really taking in how much it had cost. By the time I was done, Jace and Cios were already outside and near the car, leaving me with Ben.

"I'm proud of you," he said. "*Anthony* would be proud of you."

I felt a calm settle in my stomach at his words, replacing some of the tightness that had been there before. My eyes watered up, and I knew I was going to cry if I didn't change the subject.

"Just don't start saying 'my queen' along with the others. I don't even have a crown yet. And I don't want our car to turn into a pumpkin or anything in the next few minutes."

Ben laughed and took my hand again. It was exactly what I'd needed to refocus. It was time to find the proof we needed.

CHAPTER TWENTY

By the time we'd driven all the way back to LA, it was the early hours of the morning. I'd tried to sleep along the way, more than a little exhausted, but I'd only managed to get short naps here and there. Ben had let me rest on his lap with my jacket under my head as a pillow. Cios drove Ben's car with Jace in the front beside him.

No one spoke as we pulled up at the address we'd found from the documents we'd stolen from the accountant. A large wall and a sturdy-looking gate protected a house shrouded in darkness. It was one of the largest properties in a neighborhood of very large houses. This man or dragon clearly had a lot of money too.

Jace moved Ben's car farther away in case there were any prying eyes nearby, and we approached on foot. I completely supported that level of caution and brought the shield and the almost useless spear that Alitas and Merrik had insisted I keep, even though I looked weird.

I couldn't sense any shadow catchers, but I wasn't going to take any chances, and despite their current state, the weapons had protected us well enough that I wasn't going to go anywhere without them.

Food and some sleep had made me feel a little stronger as well, although I hadn't gotten enough sleep for the long term. It was good enough for now, and I had something to focus on.

We approached the gate with me in the lead.

I pressed the buzzer, hoping the guy inside wouldn't mind too much that we were waking him so early. After a minute or so I pressed it again, holding it down longer.

When there was still no response a couple more minutes after that, I reached out a third time, but Jace beat me to it. She stuffed her finger over it and held it down for ages, and then pulsed it for even longer.

"Well, that should wake him up if he is sleeping," Ben muttered, before stepping toward the gate to examine it with the light from his phone.

There was still no answer, and Ben couldn't easily find a way through the gate from this side, not without some kind of tool. Cios joined in, trying to get the gate open, both of them rattling the solid wooden object in its frame a couple of times. It wasn't budging.

"If we're going to find proof, we need to get inside and figure out where this guy is or if he's got any documents that might serve as evidence," Jace pointed out when we all gave up and stepped back.

"Okay, then it's simple. We fly over the gate and find a way into the house," I proposed.

"We can't take dragon form outside the city," Ben replied.

I'd expected him to object, but I was surprised when Jace and Cios also hesitated.

"Taking dragon form is a huge risk somewhere like this. If we're seen by someone who thinks to grab their phone..." Jace didn't finish.

Frowning, I considered our options. I couldn't think of another way to get past the gate without going away and finding specialist locksmith's tools, and that would draw attention in other ways, not to mention how horribly wrong it could go.

There was no way I could ask the others to take this risk, however. I stepped back and made sure I had space in the road to transform without having car parts and debris become part of my body, but I jumped as I transformed, just in case.

Thankfully, I'd had enough practice at this part, at least, and I was quickly in dragon form flying up and over their heads and the gate. There wasn't a lot of space on the other side of the gate, so I was forced to transform again as I landed, something I was still learning.

I got it mostly right, but clearly panicked a little sooner than I should have. I dropped the last few feet in human form and jarred my body as I landed and crouched. The pain passed quickly, and I got back to my feet. Grinning, I went back to the gate and looked for some kind of button or switch that would open it and admit the others.

Using my hand as a light, I searched around the edge, eventually finding a set of buttons. I pressed the top one, but nothing happened, then I tried the bottom. There was a clank and then suddenly the gate started swinging open.

"Nicely done." Jace smiled as she was the first to slip through.

I returned the grin as Ben and Cios quickly followed. Before the gate had gone all the way I tried the top button again. It immediately stopped in its tracks and swung back the other way. Although I worried that it would make a lot of noise, it slid closed gently enough that it didn't make a sound, with the exception of a very faint clang when a bolt slid into place to hold it shut.

Turning to face the next obstacle with my three companions beside me, I could finally appreciate how large the house was. There were more windows than I could count at a glance, and it was four stories high. It had a slightly Gothic design, probably one of the older houses in the area, but it was well maintained and the flowerbeds, bushes, and trees around it were all manicured and free of weeds.

Whoever lived here, they had money and they were house-proud.

I approached the front door and knocked on it, although I did so gently, not entirely sure that I wanted to wake whoever might be inside anymore. There was no response, and no lights came on anywhere inside.

"Looks like they're not in," Jace observed. "You clearly haven't had a problem with breaking the rules this far. How do you feel about breaking and entering further?"

I frowned, unsure. Noticing the look on Ben's face only made me more worried that this wasn't the right thing to do. But how was I going to get the proof I needed otherwise? There was no other way.

"If you do this, bear in mind that you break even more

rules. I know that this means a lot to you, but we could just come back another day." Ben stayed my hand as I went to try a window near the door.

"We could, and I know it could be a slippery slope. I don't want to ignore my conscience. But we don't know how long we have, if this guy is in trouble like Anthony was, or if he's deliberately not answering because he doesn't realize who I am. Or he does."

Ben exhaled and ran a hand through his hair.

"Okay. I've been alongside you every step so far. But only because this guy could be in as much trouble for protecting you as Anthony was."

"Reasoning noted," I replied. "But let's hope I'm wrong."

I tried the nearest window. It wouldn't budge. Jace tried the one on the other side of the door but also got no luck. Moving in pairs and going out in opposite directions, we tried all the windows, one after the other. I was almost all the way around the back of the house, a passage making it accessible from my side, when I noticed another door.

I tried the handle without really thinking and was surprised to find it opened. Glancing at Ben and seeing a similar look of shock on his face, I paused.

Could we really just walk straight in?

"Stay here," he whispered. "I should get the others and we should all go in together. Just in case."

He barely waited for me to acknowledge his words before he moved off, but I had no intention of arguing with having backup. Going in alone was not something I wanted to do.

While I waited for him to come back with my small team, I peeked inside. It appeared to be some kind of utility room, and I feared that the door on the other side would be locked instead.

Thankfully Ben didn't take long to return with Jace and Cios. They walked as quietly as they could. As soon as they joined me, I lifted the shield and spear and moved inside.

Needing something to help me see so I didn't trip, I made the outer level of the shield glow just a little and cast a soft light forward. It illuminated a tiled floor and the clear path to the door beyond.

I approached it, and this time Ben reached forward to try the handle, allowing me to keep my weapon and shield up in a defensive position for all of us.

The door opened, admitting us into the heart of the building. We came into a large kitchen where everything was clean and tidy. Whoever lived here was definitely invested in their house. Or they had someone who cleaned and tidied up after them. With this much money, either was a good possibility.

There was no one here. In the absence of a person we could talk to, I thought we should be looking for some kind of paperwork. We would have to sweep the whole house and come back to anything that looked interesting.

I slowly led the way, the house sprawling but soon revealing a library. Jace went to investigate the desk immediately, but I stopped her and called her back to me.

"We should see if he's here first. Check he's safe and then worry about gathering evidence," I whispered.

"And what if he doesn't want us to be here? What if he doesn't want to give us any evidence?"

"There's four of us and it doesn't look like anyone else is here. How would he stop us from overpowering him and taking it? And if we come across others, we can backtrack and get our evidence."

It wasn't a perfect answer, and Jace opened her mouth to argue with me over it before throwing her hands up in the air.

"Okay. We'll do this your way."

Grateful this hadn't turned into an argument, I moved on, checking the dining room, living room, conservatory, and what also appeared to be a billiards room before returning to a set of ornate wooden stairs that curled around one side of the hallway at the front of the house and led up to the next floor.

The stairs creaked underfoot a few times, none of us getting away with moving silently upward, but still there was no sign of life. The landing showed another set of stairs that curled around on the opposite side and went up to the next floor. Cios crouched at the bottom of this to guard our rear while we swept another floor.

I went from bedroom to bedroom with Jace and Ben, checking inside each and every one and all the en suite bathrooms, walk-in closets and any other door that might have held someone on the other side of it.

It felt as if it took a tense age, constantly expecting to find someone hiding in some kind of cupboard or asleep in bed.

The third floor was much the same. Cios kept us safe from anyone else who might be in the house while we combed the place. I'd never done anything even remotely like this, but I got the impression that the majority of the house wasn't lived in. There were no toothbrushes in the bathrooms, no shampoos and no accessories like phone chargers, hairbrushes, or makeup.

It was almost like a show home, with everything tucked out of sight.

As we went up onto the final floor, our entire group together, I was sure we would find someone or some sign that someone lived here. There had been books in the study and a desk. I wished I had checked the fridge to see if there was any fresh food inside, wondering if I'd have learned if the place was inhabited quicker that way.

In some ways it was helpful not to find anyone, but a part of me wanted to come across a person. If for no other reason than I wanted a face for the secret entity that had been supporting me financially for so long.

The rooms on the top floor were smaller and condensed, the tapered roof taking away some of the space and making it easier to finish searching. Although we finally found a room that appeared used, with clothes in the closet, a toothbrush charger plugged in at a wall socket in the bathroom, and a bed that wasn't perfectly made, there was still no sign of the occupant.

When we had checked the final room and still not found anyone, all of us visibly relaxed and I straightened slightly, feeling the ache in my legs from walking so much in one night and the strain in my arms from doing it all while carrying a shield and spear in a defensive position.

"We should get back down to the library and see what we can find," Jace insisted, the most eager of us.

I knew she was right, but I could tell that Ben was still very uneasy.

"What's the problem?" I asked him under my breath as

we walked back downstairs. Jace and Cios moved faster and farther ahead. None of us were trying to be quiet anymore.

"If he's really not here, where is he?" Ben asked. "Do you think he's been chased away like Anthony had?"

"When Anthony was chased away, his place was wrecked. Completely trashed. This place is perfectly tidy. It's as if he left of his own accord." I kept my voice as low as Ben's so Jace and Cios wouldn't hear us.

"Then we really should come back later. We can get these two to keep an eye on the place instead. I don't think we should go looking through what's here."

I was starting to feel uneasy enough about being in the house and creeping around that I wasn't sure I wanted to carry on either.

Before we could get to the bottom floor, we heard a bang from something downstairs, as if someone had dropped something heavy or a door had shut with force.

Instantly, the others froze. I moved as quietly and as quickly as I could toward the front of the group, the uneasy feeling in the back of my head growing until I recognized it.

Shadow catchers.

CHAPTER TWENTY-ONE

I moved slower, fear making my blood run cold. I didn't know how many more shadow catchers I could face, but they were out in the city somewhere and I had something else in the house with us. Something I could also sense, but not in the same way.

Making my way downward, I could just about feel it moving through the house. It was in the library we had been in earlier, and that had me more worried. As I got closer, I reduced the light in my shield, hiding us in darkness and moving even slower.

If my companions wondered how I knew where to go and why I wasn't checking other rooms, they didn't say anything and simply followed, trusting me. Given my track record of keeping them safe so far, I wasn't surprised.

Whatever was ahead felt both like a shadow catcher and not. It was a confusing feeling that almost pulsed and faded, especially as I got closer and could feel it better.

After glancing back to check the others were with me, I hurried into the library. I gasped when I spotted the person on the other side of the desk, and he quickly shut a journal of some kind with a snap.

Fintar.

I'd not been able to sense him either of the previous times we had met, but for some reason I could now. It didn't make any sense.

"Hello, Scarlet." I was sure I hadn't given him my name. Then I remembered that he had claimed to know me. Had also claimed to know Anthony.

"What are you doing here?" I asked, lowering the shield I carried only slightly. I moved into the room just enough that my companions could join me and I could show force.

At the back of my mind, I felt the increasing threat from beyond. There were more than three shadow catchers coming our way, and now I was so close to Fintar, I was fairly sure that he was somehow connected to them. Was he controlling them? And if so, why hadn't I felt it before?

"I'm looking for information, much as I would guess you are, given the company you have with you. But I haven't found what I seek."

"What are you seeking? Maybe I've seen it." I was willing to pretend to be allies for now while he was being civil. There was a chance he didn't realize I could feel his connection.

I moved closer, lowering the shield and spear.

My friends spread out a little, though a single glance at Ben was enough to keep him by my side.

"I am seeking an answer to a very important question."

"Cryptic."

"What do you seek?"

"An answer to a very important question as well. Although, mostly, the person who lives here. I have a feeling you might know where they are better than you're letting on."

Jace looked up from the books she was browsing on a shelf.

"What's going on?" she asked.

"Scarlet here is a lot more perceptive than she appears. Why don't you tell them what you can feel?"

"Shadow catchers. Lots of them, coming this way. But not because I'm attracting them. Has it ever been because I was attracting them? Or has it always been because of you?" I gritted my teeth, wanting to smack this guy and wipe the smug smile off his face.

"You're a handler?" Ben drew closer to me.

Fintar stepped back as he lifted his hands in a 'you caught me and I'm not particularly bothered about it' expression.

"Sometimes they come because they sense you. They've always been more drawn to red dragons, but they weakly sense us all."

"How long have you served the demon behind the gate?" I asked.

"I don't serve anyone. That's what you red dragons have never understood. But of course, you already believe you're the next queen. Well, there's no proof of it. None here. The guy who lives here isn't your benefactor, nor is he the person putting money into your trust fund. It's some wealthy heir to a Fortune 500 company. Some brat who travels and wastes his parents' money."

"How do you know that I came here looking for my

benefactor?" I demanded, feeling the shadow catchers getting ever closer, so many of them now that we were going to be in trouble if we didn't get out soon.

"You're getting information from us, aren't you?" Jace asked, coming forward. It was only as she spoke that I noticed Cios was missing. Had he not come into the room with us, or had I not noticed him leave?

I was more than a little confused. Something was going on here that was bigger than I could understand. And I couldn't even be sure that this guy was telling the truth.

"Put the journal you're holding down and step away from the desk." I decided I couldn't take the chance of believing him. With the shadow catchers now only about half a mile from the house and closing fast, I only had a couple more minutes at most to figure it out. I lifted the shield and spear again.

"I can't do that," he replied as Jace and Ben put their hands on my shoulders, lending me their power.

"I'm not asking nicely," I insisted, beginning to channel the power from my two friends and myself into both the shield and spear.

Despite how old the man looked and how he had clutched his cane the entire time, he turned and ran toward the nearest window with the strength of a twenty-something man.

Yelling in fury and not really thinking about the consequences of my actions, I threw the charged spear at him. It struck his shoulder, making him grunt as electricity crackled across his skin and he dropped the journal he had been holding.

As a group of three, we rushed forward. Ben grabbed

the end of the spear again, Jace went for the journal, and I tried to stop our quarry from leaving before I was done with him.

Two of the three of us succeeded. Jace got the journal and lifted it up as Ben got a grip on the very end of the spear. It made a sickening sound as it came free from the man's flesh.

At the same time, I grabbed at him and found his arm. Within half a second, something stung my hand so badly that I loosened my grip. Before long I was holding only fabric as it decayed in the palm of my hand, burning it and smoking as the remainder of the spear did.

Another second later, the creature, whatever he was, crashed through the back window, shattering glass everywhere but somehow continuing to run. There was no way we would catch him now. Not when he was running straight to the shadow catchers.

"He's not a dragon." I was stunned at seeing the spear and clothes suddenly react the way everything did to shadow catchers. The pain in my hand was already starting to fade, thankfully buffered by the clothes. It merely looked a little singed.

"He is...sort of." Jace tucked the journal into a pocket and ran to the desk to try to see what he had been looking at when we'd interrupted him.

"He's part demon, part dragon. Gifted some of the shadow catcher abilities and their longer life in return for having to obey an order or two now and then." Ben looked disgusted as he spoke and handed me back the final chunk that remained of the spear.

It was now barely the length of a wooden dagger, but it

was still better than nothing. I gripped it tightly and looked for the best way out. Jace was still pulling out drawers and looking through bits of paper as Ben joined her.

"We don't have time." I felt the shadow catchers hurtling toward us. We would already find it very hard to escape from the area without running into at least a few of them.

"You're the heir and he knew it. We need to make sure we have all the proof there is here," Jace exclaimed as she and Ben searched even more frantically.

I wanted to scream in fury and frustration. They were right, and all I could do was step forward and help.

"What was in the journal?" I asked as I pulled out what looked like car maintenance bills. These weren't going to prove anything.

"A diary. But it's not enough." Jace pulled out another stack of documents and slammed them down on the desk to look through them. I helped her, but it seemed as if our duplicitous helper from earlier had been right about one thing. These documents were for someone entirely different. So where had the journal come from?

I stepped back and looked around, not sure what I'd see, but Cios ran into the room as I felt the shadow catchers slow slightly. It was too late. We had to get out.

"Help from our crew is on the way. I've told them we have the dragon heir with us and that we are convinced of it but we need aid."

Jace set her jaw as if she didn't entirely approve of him divulging something like this, but it was done now, and we'd need their help. We were surrounded by shadow catchers, and we still didn't have what we needed.

"It's really time to go." I took a closer look at the window to see if we could exit that way. There was too much broken glass and the remaining shards looked like they were dripping an opaque substance—could that be acid? Involuntarily, I flexed my singed hand.

Bringing the shield and spear together in a defensive position again, I nodded at my three companions and they formed up behind me once more. We were going to have to fight our way out. I could only hope that we had enough strength left after the long day.

It took me so long to get through the rest of the house and into the kitchen that by the time we reached it, I felt all the shadow catchers around the walls of the back and front yard.

I felt gratitude for the walls and the very gate that had kept us from getting in right away. They were buying us more time now. I hesitated in the kitchen, my eyes fixing on a rack of kitchen knives sitting on the surface in one corner.

Cios followed my gaze and grinned before running over to grab the whole wooden block.

"Worth a try," I agreed, leading the three of them on.

"The spear helped when you threw it," Ben agreed. It was logic all of us could get behind. And I wasn't going to be fussy when I was carrying a spear that had gotten shorter with every successful hit on the enemy. It was a tough battle when the very weapon I carried was slowly decaying away, despite the powers we'd infused it with.

I felt nerves ripple through me as I noticed there were at least six distinctive shadow catcher presences in my mind. We'd never faced odds this bad before. Admittedly, the last few weeks had been anything but normal, so I was beginning to think I shouldn't find anything surprising anymore.

Instead of leading my group around to the front of the house where it felt as if three of the demonic creatures were concentrated, I led them further around the back of the house, to a lawn and more well-kept trees. I had wondered if the owner had cared for them himself, but I was starting to get the impression that was the work of a professional.

I already suspected that my benefactor had never lived here at all, but then, was it possible that others had access to this property for various other reasons? My thoughts turned to the journal we'd rescued from Fintar as he fled. We'd have to have a better look at it later.

Pushing the confusing thoughts from my head, I tried to focus on the problem at hand. The shadow catchers were starting to decay their way in through the walls, eating up the bricks and making a stench that made me wrinkle up my nose in disgust.

And we needed to get out of the center of them and around to the car at the front of the house. No easy task. Not sure what else to do but go on the offensive and try to even the odds, I used what I could feel to make my way toward one of the monsters at the side of the house.

I heard it as it worked its way toward us, going through what it couldn't get around. The stench of decay and rot grew worse, but I concentrated on what I needed to do and pulled on the energy of the three dragons with me, combining it with mine and preparing to hurl the monster back.

I waited for the perfect moment to attack, the shield ready to defend us and my spear ready to strike. For a few tense seconds, my heart pounded in my ears and chest as I focused on my breathing and feeling my magic flow. So close now.

As soon as the wall in front of me crumbled away enough that I could see a hint of movement, I stabbed forward with the spear. Shards of brick went flying, caught between the demonic creature and my power. Some chunks clattered on the shield, but most went forward and toward the shadow catcher.

My spear hit it as well, making it screech twice and sending a shock wave up my arm. I gritted my teeth against the pain and pulled the spear back.

It broke off, leaving the bulk of it inside the creature and giving me a smoking hilt. It wasn't going to be of any more use, so I dropped it and pulled one of the smaller knives from the block.

"Anyone know how to knife-throw?" I asked. More of the wall tumbled down as the monster flailed in pain and continued to rot and decay anything it came into contact with.

"Hold it by the hilt and flick your wrist. Try not to make it spin." Cios was the only one who responded, and I was going to have to learn fast. None of the rest of them could make this work. With any luck, the energy I pumped the blade with would hurt the creatures even if I was unable to throw it well.

Surely all it had to do was hit?

I felt and saw the shadow catcher on the other side of the wall recover a little. I was about to find out.

CHAPTER TWENTY-TWO

Time seemed to stand still as the shadow catcher rushed me. I held my ground, shifting the large shield to block the attack. This wasn't what I'd been expecting, but it was charged with our power, and I had to see if I could take a hit from one of them at some point.

There was a resounding clang, and I was almost knocked backward off my feet. Ben and Cios braced me as Jace reached for another knife.

I didn't give the creature time to recover, throwing the blade I already carried while Jace used the knife she had to attack the wall some more and make the hole big enough for us to escape through.

My second was so far off the mark, barely grazing the beast, that I winced, and knew I needed to make the next one count. But the combined damage of the spear, shield, and charged blades seemed to be finally working, despite the delay. The shadow catcher slowly dissolved, evaporating like hand sanitizer on a hot day.

We all blinked and stopped, none of us believing what

we'd just seen. That was something none of us had expected. We hadn't just hurt or stunned the shadow catcher. It was dead. Gone.

Not wanting to waste the time we'd gained, I grabbed another knife and helped Jace knock out the loose and unstable bricks to widen the hole.

I felt more shadow catchers working their way toward us. The nearest ones on either side came toward the hole we had made rather than creating another of their own.

My arm was already beginning to hurt and make it harder for me to keep pulling magic from my friends to combine with my own. I wasn't used to all this magic use in one day, and I had been concentrating more than normal. But there were still a lot more to fight, and they moved faster than we did.

I did the only thing I could do: continue to fight for my life.

As soon as the hole was wide enough for us to all squeeze through, I moved closer and put the shield through first. I lost connection with the dragons behind me, but somehow I could keep drawing on their energy, as if the tether that had been created between us was now so strong that it couldn't be broken by distance or a lack of contact.

I barely had a chance to straighten before another creature attacked me. This time I tried to move the shield in the way and hoped it would hurt itself, but it missed me altogether and its beak sliced through nothing but air near my head.

Relief washed through me at seeing I'd survived the attack, even if just barely. I stabbed with the knife, trying to aim truer as it reared back to lunge again. It worked. My blade slashed at it rather than impaled it, but at least it hurt the shadow catcher.

As my friends joined me, I took another step forward and struck again. Once more, I came close to being hit by the creature, but I managed to hurt it again, getting a better cut this time. To follow, I hit it with the shield, pushing it back and prepared for the way it recoiled.

"You're doing it. You're wrecking these things," Jace called. The excitement in her voice was clear, but I couldn't share her enthusiasm.

I was already very tired, and this fight wasn't over. Even if I defeated this one, another was coming up fast behind us and there were another three at least after that. I couldn't kill them all.

I was going to have to turn to defend against another, so I put all my focus into charging the blade I carried then hurled it at the wounded monster. The shadow catcher staggered back, the blade hitting better and lodging in the floating shadow.

While it flailed in pain, I whirled, and Jace, Ben, and Cios had to come around with me. I was just in time to block the next shadow catcher with the shield and stop it from hitting Ben in the back.

I winced as the pain of each brute-force attack on my shield grew and made me struggle even more.

Before I could recover and grab another blade from the block, another person appeared, coming from a small lane behind the shadow catcher. Although it was a lone dragon, she threw her weapon and it hit the creature perfectly. It also crackled a little, but it didn't do much damage. Almost immediately, the shadow catcher decayed that projectile as well, making short work of it.

Wanting to scream at the sheer futility of it all and how little anyone could help me, I took another knife and did my best to charge the shield once more. I grew light-headed but Jace reached for leaves and twigs, pulled them off the trees and bushes and hurled them at the monster in a whirlpool of debris to distract it.

Although it decayed those too, it diverted its focus and bought me a little more time. Moving with Cios and Ben, I lunged, hitting this shadow catcher with shield and blade at the same time as Jace and the newcomer threw more debris. It screeched more loudly than anything I'd ever heard before but didn't dissipate or retreat.

I let out a frustrated whimper and heard Ben shout something as he pulled me around and tried to duck out of the way. Cios moved faster than I could, pushing Ben back and saving his life. The shadow catcher's beak plunged into the outstretched arm of Cios instead. I yelled as he grunted in pain and his flesh started to rot.

With the shield barely charged, I thrust at the shadow catcher again. It drove the creature back, hurting it more and making it writhe in pain, but I was too distracted to finish it off. More people showed up then, someone reaching out to pull Cios away from me.

"All of you to us," Jace yelled. "She can channel our magic and kill these things."

None of them needed to be told twice. They rushed to my side as Jace motioned for them to get behind me.

"Move with her and keep physical contact if you can,

although she might not need it to be perfect anymore. And preferably one of each type of dragon."

I took a deep breath, trying to will my body to continue fighting and draw on the reinforcements I had, but I felt myself weakening with each attack I made and each time I had to charge the shield or a weapon.

On top of that, my hand was hurting again, and we still had two shadow catchers bearing down on us, though both were now clearly injured.

They came at us both at once, my shield and blade now guarding a group of six dragons, but the power I could draw on had also grown.

"Close your eyes," I yelled at my group as I not only hit the brightest light I could muster but thrust forward at the screeching, pained monsters. My shield hit one of them and I buried the knife handle-deep into the other.

Within moments they had both evaporated. I dropped the smoking knife onto the ground as I sagged, my vision blurring.

Ben caught me, his arms wrapping around my body as he helped lower me and give me room. He took the shield, holding it over us.

"There's at least three more shadow catchers," I warned as I tried to get my breath back and clear my head. "There also seems to be a handler out there. I think he is calling up more of them."

I frowned and tried to stand again, but Ben put downward pressure on my shoulders as all the dragons gathered, all on one knee and around me like some sort of protective ring.

"We need to try to get out of here." I looked at him, not sure I could fight any more shadow catchers like this.

"Using our powers shouldn't drain you like this," one of the new dragons said. "If you are truly the royal line and this is your birthright, it should sustain you and aid you too. Draw from us to strengthen yourself to fight on. We are all right here and willing. We've all longed for the day we could send one of these creatures back to the hell they spawned from."

As one, they all reached back toward me, still looking outward at possible threats while they connected to me. Ben grinned and nodded, and added his hand to the pile.

Taking a deep breath, I closed my eyes and tried to imagine their power flowing into me. Had I been using lots of mine to fuel the attacks and only taking the bare minimum I needed from them to do so? Almost certainly. I'd been aware of how it felt to take from them. How it felt as if I was robbing them, but I was the only one who could get us out of this mess.

At first it only felt like a tentative trickle, my conscience barely letting me take anything from any of them and my own tiredness and exhaustion preventing sense from overriding it, but my head began to clear, and my heart rate slowed. When I looked around and saw none of them in any distress, I pulled a little faster.

It was a strange sensation, knowing I was taking their power for myself and growing stronger off it, and it worried me quickly. I felt as if I could heal any hurt, put right any wrong, and suck power from them until my body not only didn't ache, but felt better than it ever had. This was something that could easily become addictive. Like a drug, giving me a high.

No sooner had I thought this than I stopped pulling on their strength entirely. I couldn't do this unless I needed it. There was no way I would use other dragons like this except to bring us together to save all of us. I had to make sure I was strong enough to resist the temptation to do anything else.

As I got to my feet, they all fell in behind me. Ben handed me my shield back while Cios held out the knife block again. I felt the remaining three shadow catchers hurrying toward our position, and I could still feel Fintar.

I wanted to get everyone out and to safety, but I also wanted to go after Fintar and find out what he knew and where he'd found the journal. But at least one of the shadow catchers was in the house, and there was still a chance my proof was in there. How did I choose between the three options?

Looking down at the shield I carried, I saw the dents in it and the way the creatures had started to break through the magic I'd charged it with over time. The front was beginning to rust here and there, as if it had been left out in the rain for too long without care.

It would still hold for several more fights—of that I was sure—but it wasn't going to last forever. It was one of the worst things about fighting these monsters. The constant need to replenish weaponry and armor because even a slight touch from one of the demonic monsters would begin to decay it.

And it seemed to happen no matter what I did with my magic. I couldn't stop it or figure out how to reverse it. I glanced at the knife block and took in how few knives we had left. I didn't really have a choice about what to do next.

I didn't have the shields or weapons to fight through lots of shadow catchers, even if I did have the power from enough dragons. And that meant I had to focus on escaping and saving everyone. My answers would have to wait for another day. One where I hadn't been tricked or set up or thwarted by someone I had thought a friend.

"Where are your vehicles?" I asked, hoping they weren't too far away and the dark would continue to help conceal us.

Two of the three shadow catchers I felt close by were still moving in our rough direction. Thankfully only one of them was between us and the direction the nearest dragon pointed in. With any luck, that meant there was only one more to take our chances with.

I led them in that direction, taking the lead as if I wasn't frightened or worried that this might go wrong. So far, I felt as if I had gotten lucky in battle, yet here I was, marching a small army toward another monster in the hope that I could defeat it in combat. At some point, people were going to suffer worse than a slash to the arm.

Despite knowing that I was going to have to fight another shadow catcher, I felt better as soon as I finished making a decision. Preparing for another battle, I started to draw on the magic around me again. I tried to be careful not to feed myself too much but at the same time keep myself able to carry on and hold the shield.

If I lost focus in a fight, it would hurt us all. And I was pretty sure someone else had said something about power and responsibility and how I needed to make sure I had both if I had either.

Feeling the shadow catchers with my mind made it easier for me to figure out where they were. If we didn't hurry forward we were going to get sandwiched between two again, which was probably what they were aiming for.

It was only as I was thinking this that I realized the creatures were being more organized and clever than they ever had been. But they also weren't going through matter in the same way. At my second encounter with the creatures, I had seen one simply pass through the door to a bar. These ones decayed everything around them instead.

The difference in behavior was more than a little confusing. I had no way of knowing for sure if this was normal or not, but none of my followers seemed to think there was anything different or unusual happening. The feeling that I was missing something wasn't going away, however.

CHAPTER TWENTY-THREE

Still unable to calm and get rid of the strange feeling in the back of my head, I slowed and considered my options.

"What is it?" Ben asked, never far away from me.

"I'm not sure. But I think that either these creatures are different, or they're being controlled by someone who is using them differently and can't seem to work out how to make them do more than decay things."

Ben lifted his eyebrows. I was going to need to elaborate. I explained as fast as I could while I changed direction and hurried my friends away purely on a hunch.

At first none of the dragons around me but Ben seemed to understand or care. I got the impression that they were as clueless as I was and hadn't noticed a pattern to the shadow catchers' behavior, which I found surprising.

"Most people run away from shadow catchers," Cios explained when I bit on my lip and tried to contemplate the possibilities and what all this might mean. Were these ones different because of who was controlling them, or was there something more going on?

My change of direction meant that I was soon facing down one of the vile monsters as I tried to rally my group once more. This one stood in between us and the strange sensation I had for Fintar in my mind. It was his line of defense.

As if it also knew that it had to be protective, this one was more wary. Where all the previous shadow catchers had fought fiercely and been incredibly aggressive, this one was more restrained. It hung back and even dodged me as I came at it.

My group was boosting me and giving me their energy to keep me from feeling faint, but I felt a responsibility to fight this fight well and not waste their life force.

Frustration started to grow in me at the strategy displayed by this new opponent, and I wasn't the only one. The dragons beside and behind me all muttered too. They were starting to realize something more was going on as well.

"Try throwing a knife again," Ben suggested when it dodged my attack for a third time and managed to duck underneath my shield and come within an inch of catching my legs.

I backed up a pace, not wanting to feel the sting of the decay these creatures could cause for a second time and aware that Cios was still grimacing in pain beside me, one arm hanging uselessly. There was nothing I could think of doing to help him while still staying focused on defending us and getting us out of this mess.

My mind was all too aware of the other shadow catchers, one of them making its way toward us, and the other still doing something nefarious inside the house. Whatever it was, it was going to be bad, and I needed to deal with this one fast.

With nothing to lose, I acted as if I was going to lunge again, but this time as the monster dodged, I followed it with my gaze, took another step back to avoid a counterattack, and hurled the charged knife at it as hard as I could.

My throwing skills were clearly getting better, as this blade lodged in the side of the creature, making it scream and squeal. I strode forward, bringing the shield perfectly in front of me while I reached to the side and hoped Cios or Ben would put another knife in my hand.

I smacked into the shadow catcher with the shield and knocked it prone, making it squeal again as both the shield and creature smoked and burned. At the same time, one of my companions handed me a blade. It was one of the larger ones and I only charged it a little while the creature writhed in agony before I slashed down at it, still using the shield as a barrier between my legs and it.

The first swipe didn't finish it off, but the second did. The shadow catcher became vapor that blew away. We all whooped, delighted, but I felt their tiredness as well. I might have reinforcements, but this prolonged fight was costing them as well.

On top of that, the shield I was using wasn't going to last much longer. Because I'd held it in the way and kept it there to protect myself, it had lost its charge again, all of it dissipating as it hit the monster. The result was that the shield had begun to decay as well.

Thankfully the rate of its decay was slower, since it was made of well-built metal, and it still held up well enough, but I worried that it wouldn't see this fight through. Especially as the feelings of unease in my mind were starting to grow again. I guessed that Fintar was trying to call up reinforcements.

We had to get this fight over and done with soon.

"I think all these shadow catchers are being controlled by someone part dragon and part whatever they are," I said as my little army fell back into formation behind me.

"Then let's take him out too." One of the newcomers gave me a small salute as I looked them all over.

There were nods and determined looks all around, even Cios making it clear he was with me.

I slowly drew on the magic again, being gentle as I felt for the strange signal Fintar appeared to be giving off now. I still wondered how I'd not picked up on it before now, but I could only assume that I'd either not been familiar enough with it to detect it, or he could mask it somehow when he wasn't controlling the monstrous creatures.

Either way, I knew of it now, and I felt him as he continued to control the two he had left nearby and summoned more from further away.

Hurrying to try to keep distance between my dragons and the other shadow catcher, and also keen to get to Fintar before he had a chance to run away, I paced forward.

It didn't take long to find Fintar, the dragon—or whatever he was—in human form, leaning on his walking stick, his eyes closed and teeth gritted. His clothes looked the worse for wear, the patch where I had grabbed at him partially decayed and now full of holes. It made me feel a little better to see that this was taxing him in some way, and he was possibly suffering. Perhaps it would give us an edge.

But any advantage we might have had vanished when his eyes snapped open. They widened as he took in how many dragons I had with me.

"No wonder you've been banishing my servants so fast. Tell me, do you like how it feels siphoning power off the dragons who will serve you?"

I was stunned by the blunt but twisted question. How did he know how it felt to draw on the power of others?

"I'm asking the questions." I knew I was deflecting and feeling more than a little guilty for it. "You know I'm the dragon heir. What proof do you have?"

"Truthfully, I wasn't sure, but I think we all know you're the dragon heir from what you've just done. I can offer you no more proof than that. And neither would I give it to you if I had any."

"Not even to save your life?"

He laughed at this, a mocking, hollow sort of laugh. At the same time his clothes suddenly decayed, all of them falling to the ground as he seemed to transform. Before long we were all staring at someone that was a cross between a shadow catcher and a human, the eyes still sort of there in a more translucent way and a body that shimmered and rippled.

I charged the shield and knife and ran toward him. I might not have the proof I wanted from him, but I wasn't going to let him get away either.

He shot some kind of blast at me when I was still several yards away. It smacked into the shield I carried, pushing me back and stunning me. It drained the charge in the shield, and me too.

While I was trying to draw on the dragons around me, he continued to back off, and the other shadow catcher from the side of the house appeared, finally reaching us.

Fintar took off as my faithful dragons positioned themselves so I was between them and danger. It gave me no choice but to face the shadow catcher. This creature was as aggressive as the first few had been, rushing me with a screech.

I didn't get the shield charged again in time but brought it around to defend myself anyway. It smoked and rusted before my eyes, but I slashed outward and over the top of it with the knife.

The creature's battle cry turned into a wounded shout, and it gave me the opportunity to back off again and gather myself. Feeling some resistance to my pull on the power from the dragons around me, I drained myself some more.

With my vision blurring a little at the edges, I launched one last attack at the shadow creature and hit it with the shield while stabbing it with the blade. It was ungainly, awkward and badly timed, but somehow I got away with it as the creature seemed disoriented.

I powered through, slashing and drawing only on what I could take from the others without resistance, as the shield slowly disintegrated in my hands and the knife smoked and curled into a blackened husk.

By the time the shadow catcher puffed into nothing and I stepped back, my head was swimming again and my weapon and shield were wrecked beyond use.

Letting go of the power in all the dragons around me, I sank to my knees. Ben's arm went around me again.

"Are there any more?" he asked.

It took all my concentration to answer his question. I couldn't feel the monsters that had been on the edge of my mind anymore and Fintar was also long gone.

"Just one in the house. I think it's destroying evidence."

"We can't fight another."

"No, we can't," I conceded.

Ben lifted me gently back to my feet, encouraging me to lean on him and let go of the weapons I was still carrying. It was all I could do to stand. My head felt light, but I heard the dragons moving around me, everyone forming up in a defensive circle again, Cios close to my other side as the only injured person.

"Can you help her along?" Jace asked Ben, and my mind struggled to process even that much. I thought he nodded, but either way, I felt the grip around my waist tighten.

We moved as one unit, and another arm came around me from the other side. The shadow catcher started to move not long after we did, as if trying to cut us off. The evil grew in my head and felt almost overwhelming.

"Hurry." I was barely able to speak through gritted teeth as I was being half-carried forward. My head was pounding and I didn't know where we were going. I didn't recognize where we were.

It wasn't long before we tumbled out onto a road. People stood on porches and by open front doors in the houses nearby.

"Hey! What do you think you're doing?" a guy yelled, but everyone ignored him as we turned in the opposite direction. Only a few seconds later, a black van pulled up and its side door slid open, revealing an interior space big enough for all of us, seats lining the opposite side of the door.

Someone reached out a hand, helping up the first dragon as we ran closer to it.

There was more yelling from one side as Ben brought me closer, and more than a few hands reached out to get me and Cios inside as well. Within seconds I sat down. Ben took the seat beside me, and someone wrapped a blanket around me. Their fingers brushed my skin as they did and I almost reached out and sucked some energy from them, wanting my head to clear.

I fought the urge, shuddering as I did. Ben only took it to mean that I was cold so put his arm around me again. Instead of giving into the urge to replenish my energy, I leaned into him and closed my eyes.

For a while I didn't care what was happening or where we were going. I just wanted to be in a vehicle that was driving away from the shadow catchers as fast as it could. We didn't go right away, though. Jace only got in when the shadow catcher appeared and came toward us. As normal humans saw it and screamed, it seemed to understand that we were no longer alone.

Instead of coming after us, it turned and hurried away. I gaped, not sure what had gotten into the creatures lately. On one hand I was grateful that they appeared to be showing some new level of intelligence so we could lure them away from people, but on the other, I was terrified of it.

As Jace finally got in, another dragon pulled the door

shut and the driver sped away. I thought I heard another round of shouting from the concerned residents, but they were entirely ignored by everyone else.

Still feeling like my head was going to explode, unable to fully sit up, I looked around at the dragons sitting with me. They were all panting hard and looking almost as bad as I felt. I had drained them all of their magical energy and we had come close to dying anyway.

How on earth was I ever going to channel enough energy to block off a gate and challenge the monster beyond it if just fighting a few shadow catchers did this to so many dragons? I really hoped there was something I was missing.

CHAPTER TWENTY-FOUR

By the time we'd been in the van an hour, I felt like I was so exhausted I could barely hold my head up, but the dragons around me were almost entirely recovered, with the exception of Cios. His arm was clearly hurting him, and I wished there was something I could do. It wasn't fair that any of them were hurting because of me.

Although I could look forward and see the road ahead, it was still dark and there weren't any streetlights. The car's headlights were only strong enough for the road ahead and to brush over the occasional tree.

After another half hour, the driver turned down a bumpy dirt road by a field, and we all had to hang on to stop ourselves from being flung around. It went on for what felt like forever to my tired body, but was probably only a few minutes. I kept looking ahead, but I couldn't see anything but more crops.

Finally, the headlights showed a large barn. The wood paneling was old but well maintained, and the sound of a barking dog was discernible in the background once the engine was switched off.

Everyone else shifted toward the door as Jace pulled it open. They filed out as if this was somewhere they expected to be, but I didn't move until only Ben and I were in the back of the van and Jace was looking up at me from the ground outside.

"You coming? I can probably get you some food and a place to rest for a bit while we wait for the others."

Ben got up at the word food. I still wasn't sure I wanted to go anywhere, especially if there was a chance I would once again attract shadow catchers, but I needed to eat and rest as well.

Knowing Detaris was safer, a huge part of me wanted to go back there now, but I didn't have my proof yet. Just the journal that Jace was walking off with as I deliberated. As I slowly stood, Ben took my hand again and helped me out of the van.

The barn wasn't the only building in the area. A large farmhouse sat across a courtyard, with a warm glow and the sound of chatter coming from the doorway. It was toward this second building that everyone was heading. Ben helped me toward it as Jace slipped inside and left the door open a crack for us.

I looked around as we walked over, feeling outward with my mind for danger even though I was shattered. Everywhere felt peaceful and calm, and there was even a feeling about the center of the farmhouse that was completely opposite to the way the shadow catchers plagued my mind. It drew me to it and helped me decide that I was doing the right thing.

It felt like safety.

As soon as I got close to the door, I could smell the heavenly scent of cooking inside, and it only made me hurry all the more. The shoe rack by the door was overflowing, far too many pairs of boots failing to fit on its shelves and working their way outward. I added mine to the pile, grateful when Ben was quick to do the same and accompany me toward the source of most of the noise.

I had only just stepped through the door into a very large farm kitchen when someone thrust a bowl of steaming hot stew at me, and a spoon. I tucked in as Ben was given another, not taking in anything else but how good it tasted until I had almost finished.

When I finally looked up, I realized that half the room was staring at me, although they were still chattering among themselves. All the people who had turned up and battled shadow catchers were there, along with several other dragons.

"Looks like you could do with seconds." Jace held out her hand to take my bowl and get me more. It broke the tension, and everyone looked back to their food or went back to helping others get theirs.

I ate the second bowl slower, finally taking in the room. It was an old rustic affair, with a well-worn large wooden table in the center. It could easily seat twelve, but only a few were sitting at it now, all of them on the far side, including Cios, who had a bandage around his arm and an easier look on his face.

"I understand what you're saying, but do you hear me?" a woman's voice came from the hall outside, loud enough we heard it from inside the kitchen. Immediately everyone went silent, all eyes turning to the door. "They haven't been through the proper protocols. Do you have any idea of the danger that—"

The woman stopped abruptly as she came through the doorway and realized we could all hear her. She was thin, older, her hair a silvery white that dangled down her back in a braid, and she had wrinkles that cut through her tanned skin.

Her gaze swept across the room and found Jace. "Report," she ordered.

"We answered a summons at the restaurant, got given the information you've just been handed that we think proves Scarlet here is the heir to the dragon throne and then took her to the gate. There and later at the house listed in the same information, she added demonstration to the written proof and fought shadow catchers, injuring and killing them. We then picked up the journal you also have." Jace pointed to the documents this new woman was carrying under her arm.

I frowned, wanting at least a quick look at those myself. I really hoped that this woman wasn't going to be difficult about letting me have that back. It was something I had helped acquire, and I needed a copy of it if nothing else.

"No one can injure or kill shadow catchers," the woman insisted.

I lifted an eyebrow. She should know that wasn't the case if the royal dragon line was supposed to have defeated the main demon and sealed him behind a gate, and all the dragon's descendants had reinforced the gate along the years.

There was a pause as Jace considered her response.

"Everyone here who saw Scarlet hurt or kill a shadow catcher in the last twelve hours, raise a hand."

Most of the room put their hands up, including the two dragons who had been in the van but hadn't joined my protective circle when the reinforcements arrived. It made me wonder what they had witnessed, but there was no way to know for sure and I wasn't interrupting whatever was happening to ask.

The older woman looked around the room, taking in every raised hand before she looked at me.

"You don't have your hand up. Don't you believe what these folks think you did?"

I was caught off guard. "Figured it went without saying that I knew what I'd killed today. You know, it's not exactly something everyone can do. It seems to have caused a bit of a stir. Not to mention those things are pretty scary. Stuff of nightmares. I'd rather not have been fighting them."

"You've got a lot of sass and confidence for someone your age."

"Apparently I've just done the impossible…" I shrugged, not sure I liked where this conversation was going and pretty sure I was going to get labeled as a typical red dragon hothead again, but I just couldn't help it. To the side of me, Ben smirked.

The woman pursed her lips.

"Sarai, think about it. Why would we lie and why would she be standing here if she wasn't who we think?" Jace asked, her voice gentle as she stepped forward.

"She's the heir, Sarai," Cios added. "You know we've handed you enough proof alone."

"With what I know of the red dragons of old, then yes,

this is enough proof," another voice said from the doorway. I looked at the source to see a man standing there, even more old and frail than Sarai. The nearest dragon who seemed to live here immediately got to his feet and pulled out a chair, angling it toward the newcomer.

"You've got more wisdom of old?" Jace asked, the respect in her voice marked. He looked at her and then at me, smiling as he did.

"Yes. I do. If nothing else, she's the spitting image of her grandmother when her grandmother used to take human form. Take a good look at her, Sarai. She's an heir."

I decided to make my case. If I didn't even attempt to steer this conversation, I had a feeling it would never go the direction I wanted. "While I'm extremely grateful that you know someone I'm descended from and have faith in me, I need proof to take back to the dragon city."

This earned me a dry chuckle from the old man.

"I don't think any amount of proof we could give you would be considered enough for them. They don't want to believe. But if you think it would help, you are welcome to all the physical evidence we have."

I nodded, not sure how to express my gratitude for the way he simply offered me everything I could possibly hope for. I wondered what additional evidence I might be able to gather, but the shadow catchers had probably trashed everything in that house by now and there wasn't anything I could do about it.

He motioned for Sarai to hold out the journal. She didn't look pleased about it, but she offered it to me eventually. I reached over to take it all, my hands trembling as I did. Was this really all the proof there was that I was the heir to a throne? It didn't look like much, and I wasn't sure it would hold enough weight with the right people, as the guy had suggested, but I guess I was going to find out.

"Can I at least take photographs of those before they disappear, possibly never to be seen again?" Jace asked.

"I was going to suggest several copies be made." Ben replied, pulling out his phone. I took mine out as the old guy motioned for the fellow who had pulled out his chair to also join in.

The four of us photographed everything, starting with the print outs of everything I had stolen from the accountant's, my proof of being the beneficiary, and then we went through the journal, page by page, making sure all four of us had clear pictures of it that could be read if necessary. It took a long time, but everyone sat around and waited as we carried out this task. Some of the dragons went back to their unfinished food, but most simply chatted and watched.

I wasn't yet fluent enough in reading the dragon language to be able to decipher much of the journal as I went, but the occasional word jumped out at me. This wasn't proof of my heritage, but it was about the magic I was supposed to be able to do. At least, that was what I thought it was about. A sort of study of the red dragon line.

Here and there I spotted what looked like hastily drawn family trees. Each one was part of some sort of narrative, words written to the sides and names repeated in the texts. I was looking forward to being able to read it properly and find out what it said. It might prove useful, even if it didn't necessarily back up the claim that I was a dragon queen.

It still seemed absolutely ridiculous to me. How could I

be a queen? But of course, even if I was, there was no way the dragon world was just going to accept it. And I didn't plan on going waltzing back in to demand a throne. If anything, Ben and I were going to have to discuss to whom and when we told all this.

Eventually, we finished taking photographs. I exhaled, realizing how completely exhausted I was, but I didn't feel safe sleeping right now. I'd been here for a while, and I was ready to leave and no longer be under a spotlight.

The sun was starting to come up on the horizon, the brighter world outside shining through the windows.

Sarai had left somewhere along the way with a couple of the other dragons, but the rest had remained. With the task done, I tucked the journal and documents into my bag.

I addressed the old man who appeared to be in charge. "If I get a chance, I'll return them to you."

"Scarlet, isn't it?" He got to his feet and came closer.

I nodded, not sure where this was leading.

"I'm Elias. I know you have a hard road ahead of you and it will sometimes seem as if you don't have the allies you deserve or need. Whatever happens and whatever it appears the world thinks, my roof will always be safe for you to shelter under. I hope my words are never tested and you never have need of it, but I know the history of your kind and I fear you will need it before the end."

"Then, thank you. So far I feel as if all I've been offered is help and understanding from people grateful to have a red dragon in the world again."

"It won't last. Be careful, Scarlet."

"She won't be alone. Wherever she goes." Ben stepped

forward and I saw the determined look on his face. He was sure of that much.

"You're the dragon Anthony spoke so highly of, aren't you? Ben."

Ben nodded but then looked down to hide a sadness that took the light out of his eyes. "I wish I could say that he talked of all of you, but he couldn't even tell me that he was working with you."

"Don't think for a second that it meant that he didn't trust you. He was a protector, and he didn't want to put you in danger if he didn't have to."

"I wish he'd left that choice up to me."

"Yes, that is often a mistake a dragon like him makes. But he would be proud of you now. Of that I am sure. You're continuing his work and doing a good job of it too. Scarlet is in good company."

Although I still had no idea who this dragon was, I could tell his words carried a lot of weight with everyone around him. I had questions for him as well, but I didn't dare ask them, as he stifled a yawn and it set off a ripple of reactions.

"We should get back to the city," Ben proposed. "My car is in LA, and I need to go back and get it, or I'll have to explain too much."

"One of our dragons moved it for you so it wouldn't get tied up in any investigation on the house we trashed last night." Jace held out his keys. "I'll take you back to it."

"You should all get some rest after that," Elias said as he shuffled away.

I watched him go, wondering if I'd ever actually be back

and if I might get to ask him what my grandmother was like.

CHAPTER TWENTY-FIVE

For the first few minutes that Jace drove, none of us spoke. Ben tilted his seat back and I curled up on the back seat, only feeling a little guilty that Jace was driving with two very tired companions. After all, I had saved her life in the last twelve hours. Although the way she had been able to call for aid had saved ours as well.

"Do you really think the city will listen to you?" Jace asked when Ben let out a small sigh as if he was uncomfortable or struggling to get some sleep despite the tiredness.

"I don't know. It will be hard to work out who knows what and whether they are deliberately hiding the state of the gate from people or they're as ignorant as we were," Ben replied, his voice low.

I kept my eyes closed, wondering if they'd mind me hearing this conversation.

A few seconds later, Jace spoke again. "Not everyone is for having a red dragon on a throne. You need to be careful whom you trust. I think Anthony had evidence or was convinced that there was someone in the city that would be a danger to Scarlet. I know that she's still naturally powerful and they know of her existence now, but she's special and I think we need to keep that from the wrong people for as long as possible."

I couldn't help but wonder who this someone might be. It wasn't as if Ben needed telling, though. He had been guarding me in all sorts of places to try to make sure that I was safe. And I now had even more reason to be very careful where I went and to whom I told what.

Someone we had trusted for a few days and appeared to fight alongside us against the shadow catchers had actually been in league with them. Had been some strange abomination himself. And I hadn't felt the threat at all until it was almost too late. There could have been a lot more danger at the house, and I had the sudden thought that there could be other handlers looking to endanger my life.

"I wish I knew what Anthony knew." Ben's voice was even quieter, as if the words came with the heft and heaviness of shame and heartache.

"Anthony knew what he did, and it still didn't keep him or Scarlet safe. You know other things and have a chance to act differently. All you can do is your best and hope that it's enough. We're all still here and she's safe enough for now."

"We shouldn't have to hide who she is."

"No. But dragons have never been the best at uniting. Neither are humans. And when you've got a demon exerting his control, and he can get into the minds of both and encourage them to do things they wouldn't otherwise do, when he can twist and manipulate and lie, we are left having to stand against those fooled by it, even when the same blood flows through our veins."

"Especially when they believe they are the ones doing what's best for the world."

"Everyone always believes they are right. It takes a lot to understand that the vast majority of the time we're wrong. That we have to learn and grow and adapt. That others deserve our respect no matter what they think."

"I think that's one of the wisest things I've heard anyone say in weeks."

"Those aren't my words. Elias. He has seen a lot and done a lot."

"Is he really as old as they say?"

Jace let out a chuckle. "Depends what they say. But probably."

"The highest I've heard is that he's coming up to a thousand years." Ben mumbled the words, clearly not sure if he should believe them, and I almost spluttered, taken aback by this revelation. Could dragons really live that long?

"Oh, no, definitely not. He's got a few hundred under his belt, but the oldest dragon in any of our records still didn't get to five hundred. And that was with the aid of magic and a very set routine."

"Good point. But either way…meeting him was…an experience. A lot of the dragons in the city think he's dead now."

Jace sighed and shook her head.

"Doesn't surprise me. Easier to think someone died than that they turned against you and condemned your actions."

I felt as if I was getting a succinct history lesson, but it ended there and Ben and Jace slipped into a companionable silence.

Despite my previous thoughts on the subject, all this speculation made me want to run away from it all. Who wanted to be an heir to a massive problem, when I could do what Jace and Cios did and lead a normal life, gossiping and hypothesizing, all the while knowing that it wouldn't change our world. It wasn't fair that I had to hear it and know it was all about me, and it was down to me to make it all better. That these people who would be benefiting from my struggles might not be accepting—or even worse, would be rejecting me, putting me in danger and making my life hell.

But I didn't give voice to any of those thoughts. The car was silent as I drifted into sleep for a while.

I didn't wake up until Jace turned off the engine and Ben reached out a hand to wake me. At first I was disoriented, my mind back in that study, hoping to replay the events in a way that would expose the evidence I needed to prove I wasn't the heir at all.

Of course, none of it was true. I woke up still very much the person I was and still somehow the heir to a throne I hadn't known existed only a month or so earlier.

Jace gave me a gentle smile and patted my hand.

"Don't be a stranger. I'll keep searching to see what I can find for you."

"Thank you." I wasn't sure what else to say. "And give Cios my best wishes for his recovery."

It was something safe to say and made them feel valued. It was the best I could do when internally I was freaking out.

As soon as we were out and walking toward our car, Jace pulled away and left us to it, which I understood. No one wanted to take any chances they didn't have to right now.

I followed Ben toward his car, noticing that it wasn't far from where we'd left it, just far enough away that it hadn't been obvious it was ours. And that meant I could see the house we'd been in overnight. In the light of day, it didn't look quite so large or foreboding. The gate was partially open and had crime scene tape over it.

With no cop cars nearby, I paused beside Ben's car, unable to look away. Ben opened the passenger door for me before he noticed what had my attention. His head swiveled between me and the house, and I saw the questions forming on his face.

"I think I have to know," I said. "I need to know if the shadow catcher was in there destroying evidence. If the guy we were looking for might have lived there."

Ben frowned and studied me, then looked around to see if the coast was clear.

"Okay, but we need to not get caught doing this."

"Then we should go around the back. And probably stop milling around beside a car we don't want identified as ours."

Ben almost growled at the attitude I gave him, but I ignored his protest and went toward the part of the sidewalk where the van had picked us all up. We had burst out from the foliage and almost immediately the van had arrived, so if I followed the grassy area away from the road I should be able to find my way back into the house.

When I'd been here last, I had been trying to get out and survive. This time I appreciated that all the pressure was off. I saw the decay and damage our attacks and theirs had done, however, and more crime tape trying to encourage me not to go in. I ignored that, sure that the police couldn't possibly understand what had happened.

I was also sure that the coast was clear this time, grateful that my mind could feel threats from so far away. It meant I was genuinely safe to explore for a while.

There was still a large decayed and broken area of the wall where the shadow catchers had tried to get to us, and yet more crime tape. To get past this section, I had to pull it away from the wall.

It was the first thing to truly make me uncomfortable. With the crime tape pulled down, there was a good chance the cops would know someone had entered the scene. All I could hope was that they wouldn't notice until I was long gone.

Ben followed me, keeping quiet but often frowning and making it clear that he didn't really want to be there. I tried not to focus on his disapproval right now.

We strode through the house, and I felt a sort of residual...*ick*...on everything. The shadow catcher had definitely done damage. The stairs were ruined, warped, and decayed almost beyond recognition. And the kitchen hadn't fared much better. I continued onward, though.

Of all the places in the building that I could check, the library was the one that was most likely to contain the proof we needed. It was also the biggest trail of rot and decay. This was where the shadow catcher had been.

As we got closer, my heart continued to sink. This wasn't going well, and it wasn't long before I could see the destruction to the whole room. There wasn't really anything left at all. Where rows of bookshelves had once stood there was now nothing but rotted piles of wood and fragments of paper that blew in the breeze from the warped and cracked windows on the far wall.

I wanted to cry as I surveyed the damage. There was nothing left to be salvaged. Even the desk was a rotted pile of wood that had collapsed in on itself, mold growing all over it.

"I'm sorry, Scarlet. I know it's not easy to see this. The lost chance of finding more evidence was the sacrifice we had to make to get out with our lives, but I think you did the right thing. You saved us all last night."

"I couldn't have done it without all the power I pulled from all of you." My voice sounded hollow as I stared at all the fluttering page fragments.

I remembered how it had felt to drain them the way I had. The power and the responsibility all at the same time. Knowing I needed to keep them safe, but that I couldn't do what was needed without taking from them. It had a duality to it that made me worried. How did I know where to draw that line?

"We should return to the city. I don't think we should tell anyone yet, even if we had undeniable proof that you are the heir." Ben took my hand. I let him hold my fingers, but I didn't tighten my grip back.

I didn't understand any of what had happened in the

last twenty-four hours, and this was something I wasn't ready to think about yet. I knew we had to go back, and I knew the elders were in denial about the gate weakening on some level. But the rest was another matter.

"Anthony was keeping me safe from the dragons in the city for some reason." I was unable to tear my eyes away.

"He was. And there could be many reasons why. He might have simply not wanted you to draw attention to yourself by discovering that you could draw on the power of all of us."

"And it might have been because someone will try to kill me the moment they find out."

"That too. And most likely the answer lies somewhere in between." Ben gave my fingers a gentle squeeze.

"There are possibly multiple reasons. I'm pretty sure that we need to be careful either way."

"I'll try to figure out why and keep looking for whoever is paying your fund out. There's a chance they'll have answers. Whoever lived in this house fled before we got here. Something spooked them."

"Do you think they have more proof?" I finally accepted that I'd done all I could for now.

"I don't know. And I don't know if it will ever matter. To some degree, I think the dragons around us will either decide to believe or not, and only some will be swayed with proof anyway."

"But we have to hope that proof will make a difference where it matters." I squeezed his hand back finally, hearing the cynicism in his words and wondering where it had come from.

"We do. Hope. That's about all we can do sometimes."

Together we turned and left, heading back out of the house and away from all the destruction. I was glad we'd come here, if for no other reason than it had shown me what I was capable of. Both for good and for evil. It had also given me the chance to make some new friends.

On a lot of levels, I was glad that I wasn't going to go straight to the elders in Detaris and tell them I was the heir to the throne. I wasn't ready for what that meant. Being any kind of leader seemed strange to me. I didn't want to lead people. I just wanted to live and eat chocolate and be a normal young woman.

I wanted to cook good food, laugh at my friends' jokes, and give the bullies in the city something to make them think twice about picking on someone different the next time.

And I wanted to fly. Anywhere and everywhere. Wherever the winds could take me.

CHAPTER TWENTY-SIX

Driving back to the city felt strange. All my belongings were in this car, and the one person I knew I could rely on, too. It felt like the end of an era more than a bright new beginning, and I was a mix of terrified, excited, and resigned. This wasn't the first time I'd been packed into a car and moved, but after I'd gotten my apartment I had vowed to myself that I'd never move again except on my terms. Now here I was, moving because I had no choice.

We had been driving for a while. I'd dozed again, encouraged by Ben on the basis that we wouldn't be able to tell anyone that I had been up all night fighting shadow catchers with exiled dragons.

"How did the city come to be led by elders?" I asked. "Are they voted on or anything?"

"The royal line decides their council and who they think can advise them best. The last king put together the group we now think of as the elders. They were his council. Well, for the most part. It's been a long time since we had an active monarch."

"For the most part?"

"When one of them dies or retires they nominate a successor, or the whole group does."

I nodded as I frowned. It was something that had good reasons for existing in the first place, but in theory it could easily become stale, or have an inherent bias introduced by the last king.

"And the last king was my father?" I only now considered what being the heir meant in relation to my parents.

"I guess he must have been. Unless he's an uncle or a cousin. But we might be able to find out for sure."

"Unless it's easy to do, I don't think it's worth our time." As much as knowing who my parents were would be good, what I really wanted to know was if I was a dragon heir, and I wanted answers to more important questions.

A part of me knew I must be the heir. How else could I do what I could do? But I wanted actual proof, and I didn't want to have to fight public opinion if I also had to fight whatever evil lurked beyond the gate.

My only comfort was that I didn't have to fight the thing behind the gate directly. It was trapped, and as long as I studied hard and learned to control what I could do and get stronger, I was going to be able to keep it stuck there for as long as I lived. After that, I didn't care.

When we drove over the edge of what looked like a cliff, I found myself holding my breath. It wasn't the first time I'd been driven over into what appeared to be nothing, but it was always a little disconcerting. What if Ben misjudged it and drove over the wrong section of the cliff?

He hadn't, however, and the city appeared in front of me. It was another thing that took my breath away. Majestic, tall, and built over water to protect it from shadow catchers, the dragon refuge was exactly as it had been the first time I'd seen it. It glistened in the sun, every tower unique and beautiful in its own way.

I watched the dragons flying around it, many using flight to get from one tower to the next, and others in human form using the different bridges that connected everything.

The water crashed around the city's base and the wind whistled through its tops. And it felt like home. Despite coming back to it feeling like I had become a different person while I had been gone, it was my home now. Everything I owned was here, as well as my new friends. I was already trying to spot them among the other dragons.

By the time Ben pulled up in the small parking lot at the base of one of the larger towers, we had drawn the attention of the small city guard and their commander. While they were always awkward about us leaving the city, they greeted us enthusiastically when we returned.

It didn't take long for me to notice that other dragons were coming in closer as well, some of the community reacting to my presence. Ben picked up on it as soon as I did.

"Looks like the elders have been waiting for our return. I've just seen one of their aides fly up to their tower." He came close and reached into the car as if he was helping me get my stuff from it so he could whisper to me. "It's possible that they've heard about the incident last night. They may question us again, but I'll try to get them to accept that we haven't been involved and don't know anything about it. You should let me do the talking if possible."

I wasn't going to argue if it meant I didn't have to try to explain this mess, especially when lying wasn't an option. Whatever we told them, if we did it in the elders' chamber, it had to be near enough to the truth that it appeared to be the truth.

I had more stuff than Ben and I could carry in one trip, but we were soon joined by Neritas and Flick, who had appeared as soon as the guards had checked over our car and waved them through.

Stuff had never mattered to me much, so between the four of us we could just about manage what was left of my possessions and the board games of Anthony's we'd decided to keep. I'd left behind all of the furniture. Everything here was so much more artistic and stylish anyway.

Neritas walked alongside me toward the first bridge. "Looks like you had a rough time of it,"

"What makes you say that?"

"The strange marks on your arm and the fact that you're wearing the same clothes you left in so many days later."

Flick smirked very briefly at that last part.

Great. These two think I smell, and I probably do.

Brenta approached us. "Scarlet, Ben, how wonderful to see you have returned to us." She saved me from having to respond to my friends but made me feel put on the spot in a whole new way. This was the elder who had proclaimed my judgment the last time I'd been before them.

"Brenta, as always, it is good to be back. You don't normally greet returning pilgrims to the city. I would have thought you'd be too busy for that. To what do we owe such an honor?" Ben managed to keep his voice light, as if he was truly pleased and grateful for such a courtesy.

"A question, and sadly not a greeting that comes with hopes. An unease about the answer I will be given."

"Then I hope we can put your mind at rest and our answer isn't what you fear. Please ask your question and let us discover either way."

It was another glib response, as if he had no idea something as dangerous as the night before might have happened.

At first Brenta didn't respond. She glanced at Flick and Neritas as they helped carry our belongings toward Ben's accommodation. None of us stopped walking, forcing her to turn and come with us.

"I need you and Scarlet to come with me to the chambers to answer this one."

"Really? To answer a single question? I was under the impression that the elders were already satisfied with Scarlet and what she knows of Anthony's disappearance."

It took all my control to appear calm and as confused as Ben looked at this point, but my heart rate was increasing. I did not want to have to go back to being scrutinized. And on top of that, my friends were now paying even closer attention.

"It doesn't involve that matter. Other city business."

"Ah, then please, feel free to ask your question down here. You know us to be truthful, and Scarlet's friends would hear of anything you asked anyway."

This made Brenta purse her lips and furrow her brow. Clearly this wasn't the response she'd expected.

"I'd normally be happy to come up, especially as you felt it necessary to ask us to, but Scarlet is still struggling to fly safely in the city, something I notice that you're striving to solve for her." Ben didn't look at Brenta as he said this last part, instead concentrating on the bridge in front of him.

I dared to glance her way and noticed that her eyes narrowed. This was seriously pissing her off, and there was a part of me that was delighted about it.

She didn't respond, instead followed us up the last few flights of stairs and the next two bridges until we arrived at the tower Ben lived in. We still had a little way to go up, but the tower was empty inside and this seemed to be enough to satisfy Brenta.

"It came to our attention this morning that shadow catchers attacked a human residence in LA last night. In much the same way that Anthony's apartment was attacked."

"Really? That's awful! It makes me wonder if there's something in the city drawing the vile creatures in. Are there many exiles there?" Ben asked.

"There are some, as there are everywhere, but I have to ask. Did you have anything to do with it?"

"Why would we help shadow catchers?" I sounded as indignant as that statement would make me.

There was a pause. Brenta had not expected that question.

"I thought they were attacking you when you left the city," Flick asked.

"They did a few times. Scariest thing I've ever had to face. If it hadn't been for the city guard the last time…" I shuddered, not having to fake that either.

"If you weren't involved...good. I would hate to have thought you were in danger in any way. Especially after, as you've already said, the events the last time you left the city. I was concerned for your safety and I'm sure the other elders will be relieved to hear that you weren't in any danger."

"No, thankfully not. I considered seeing some of my human friends from my life before, but I didn't in the end. Ben didn't think it wise either, so we simply tidied and cleaned the two apartments and brought back everything we're keeping." It was enough truth that I didn't feel like I was lying this time. It almost made me grateful that Ben had been so awkward about me seeing my friends. I could be far more honest about it now.

This seemed to be the final comment needed to satisfy Brenta. She nodded and hurried away, not apologizing for any of the suspicion she'd disguised as concern.

By the time we got the boxes and bags up to Ben's rooms, I was exhausted and my stomach was rumbling loudly enough that Flick laughed.

"Sounds like you've missed the burgers here," Neritas observed. "It's not long until lunch. We could probably fix that."

"Yes. Go, eat and then go to classes, before more of the elders assume that I am the worst guardian known to all dragons and keep dragging you off into danger and neglecting you." Ben put down his box, the heaviest one that had contained more of Anthony's belongings.

I got the feeling that he wanted to go through it himself and put it all somewhere safe, but we didn't have much space to spare right now. On top of that, lunch did sound amazing.

Escorted by my two friends and relieved to be somewhere else, I almost felt like a normal young woman again, eager to go back to classes and settle into life in this world.

Although I thought they had just been trying to help me give Ben space, as soon as we all sat down with food in a tucked-away section of the restaurant, early enough it was still practically empty, Neritas leaned in closer.

"Okay. Come on, Red. Tell us what really happened while you were out there."

I was too surprised by the question to hide my shock at the implied knowledge behind it. How had they known?

"We took bets on whether there would be another big event in LA while you were gone or not. Just between a few of us, mind. Found enough people who didn't want to think there might be something special about you. They bet against us just to try to piss us off."

"I'm not sure I want loads of dragons knowing that something happened," I protested.

"Oh, it's okay. The elders may have to accept that you're telling the truth unless they're willing to actually claim you're liars in front of everyone, but we all know that if something happened while you weren't here, chances are you were involved. In reality they know it too. They're just having to save face."

"It's a pretty cynical point of view, but for once I agree with Neritas," Flick added.

While I thought about what to say, the two of them dug into their food and waited. Both of them kept looking at me as if they expected me to gather myself and then tell them. Neither of them thought I might try to hide what I said for a second.

"If I tell you what happened I might be putting you both in danger as well." I wasn't sure how true it was, but it was enough that it made me worried.

"Red, the moment we decided to be friends with you rather than bully you like everyone else, we accepted we were okay with any danger around you. When are you going to start understanding that?" Neritas frowned and took another bite of his burger.

"Okay, I know. I just…it could get…really dangerous. And I don't exactly have a lot of friends."

"We appreciate that you don't just consider us expendable, but you let us worry about us and tell us what's really going on. The information is safe with us, and we'll make sure you're as safe as you can be more effectively if we know what else we're facing on top of the city bullies."

Flick had a good point. I hadn't been intending to tell them the truth, but in that moment I knew I had to. They were risking their lives for me and had already done so in the past. Both of them had given so much to help me already. If I had any integrity, I had to repay that level of commitment with some kind of trust.

I tried to gather my thoughts. "Okay. Turns out the elders are either lying or in denial about the gate and a whole bunch of other stuff. And only the heir to the throne can save the entire world."

Neritas chuckled before he realized I was serious.

"That bad, huh, Red?"

"Possibly worse."

"Then we really better know. Sounds like you need all

the allies you can get." Flick looked serious—a rare occasion—and it spurred me on to spill all the beans. I spent the next hour telling them everything that had happened to me on this trip and the last two out of the city.

I kept a few details to myself. That Anthony had left a journal for me and that I had met Elias. But I told them everything around it and did my best to never lie. It was the best I could do under the circumstances.

Both of them listened and only asked a question now and then to get extra info or make sure they understood something. Finally I exhaled and nodded, done and pretty exhausted for having told so much at once.

Neritas sat back. "So, we're in the presence of royalty."

"Don't say it like that. There's not enough evidence to prove it and I don't want to be royalty." I frowned.

"You don't have to want to be a princess to be one. It's like being a color. It just is what you are. It's in your blood. And we all know that you're a powerful dragon. If you're not the royal line, you're from one of the strong rebel lines. And they're known for claiming they're royalty, so either way you might as well claim to be a princess and say it's in your blood."

"He has a point," Flick added. "You wouldn't be lying."

"Neither of you are freaked out by this?" I asked.

"Not really. It's nothing dragons haven't faced before." Neritas took one last swig of his drink, finishing the soda and leaving the last of the ice.

I looked between the two dragons, realizing for the first time that they were right. If the stories of what previous dragons had faced were true, then none of this was new. And there was a sort of comfort to knowing that I wasn't the first to face a particular struggle. Especially as all the dragons who had faced this gate problem before me must have succeeded.

So far, we had a one hundred percent success rate. And that was a happy thought.

EPILOGUE

Almost an entire week had passed since Ben and I had got back into the dragon city, and I was already starting to wish that I could leave again. Neritas and Flick thought it was funny, but they would. They'd made a small fortune off the back of my last run-in with shadow catchers and listened to my fears and worries about what it meant for all our futures.

One of the biggest fears I had was partially solved by the journal we'd begun looking through. It talked of techniques I could use to get more power out of myself and other dragons when channeling power to fight shadow catchers, but it was vague in a lot of places.

And on top of that, I couldn't exactly practice it in my classes or ask a teacher to help. I shouldn't even know how to do this sort of thing. It was something no one talked about, and it was considered unnecessary for any red dragon to learn now that the gate was in place. And to challenge that narrative would show something had happened to open my eyes.

When I'd expressed this to Neritas and Flick a couple of times, they suggested we try to find somewhere to practice with just the three of us. Or even rope Ben in as well. I'd resisted this, not wanting to take the risk when, as far as we were aware, there could be an easy way to prove my heritage soon anyway.

I was pretty sure the elders were keeping an eye on me now. A familiar-looking dragon was often in the skies nearby when I had my flying lessons. The upside of that was that I hadn't had anyone engage in dangerous tactics around me or try to get me to crash.

But no matter how much I tried to be positive, I couldn't shake the feeling that I ought to be doing more. I didn't know how much more the gate could handle, and Ben hadn't yet had any luck working with Elias to get more information on the true whereabouts of my mysterious benefactor, the only person who could prove I was the heir.

Sighing, I threw myself down on the comfiest seat in Ben's little house, once more agonizing over whether I should be training or not. I picked up the journal I'd acquired from the house before Fintar had used his shadow catchers to ruin everything. Ben had been translating it for me, and his notes were beside the open journal.

I flicked through them now, reading about some interesting combinations of just two different dragon abilities, how they could be effective in certain situations, and then there was a tiny section on all of them combined. It basically said, "Used to kill the enemy."

"Helpful," I said aloud.

Ben came through the door. "What's helpful?"

"This journal." I waved the newest translated sheet.

"There's some good stuff in there..." Ben sat in a chair nearby, one hand tucked into a pocket. "I think the next few bits might help. But only if you're willing to try to practice."

I frowned, still not wanting to tell him my biggest reason for being against regularly pulling power from others. A part of me was hoping the book would talk about it and how it could be managed. So far, I'd had no luck.

"Anyway, I've got something else. Haven't looked at it yet, but I managed to find someone by the same name as your benefactor. Right sort of age too."

"Why didn't you say?" I leaned forward as he pulled out a letter.

"I wasn't sure they'd respond, and I knew I couldn't use normal tech to talk to them."

Ben pulled it from the envelope and started skimming it. His eyes lit up and he began to grin.

"Read it out loud, please," I asked him

"Okay. There's the usual 'thanks for your letter and I appreciate you being subtle about this.' Then, 'I can confirm that I'm the person you're looking for. While I don't know if I have exactly what you need to prove something beyond a reasonable doubt, I do know a few possible sources. I was convinced once upon a time, and there should be proof. None of this can be discussed in a letter, however, and some care would have to be taken to ensure that the events of last week weren't repeated. Perhaps we can agree on something mutually beneficial in a few days.' Then there's a few suggested times, and finally, 'In the words of our late friend Anthony, may we all live long enough to see the sun come up in the sky twice in one day and the moon always shine on our dreams,' which is something I'd forgotten he said."

By the time he'd finished I was grinning like a Cheshire cat, and I felt it. Not only did we have a lead again, but we had another phrase to help us translate Anthony's journal.

Ben looked at me, the shine in his eyes matching my own. It wasn't a lot to work with and might lead to a dead end again, but we weren't out of this fight yet, and it gave us the one thing we'd really needed: hope.

THE STORY CONTINUES

The story continues with *Dragon Revealed*, coming soon to Amazon and Kindle Unlimited.

Claim your copy today!

ACKNOWLEDGMENTS

This book was a little delayed on when I hoped to get it to all of you darling readers. Life sometimes doesn't go the way it's planned. I have had a rocky 18 months or so but I'm very glad I can finally bring this one to you all. I hope you'll forgive the lateness and enjoy the journey that Scarlet goes on next.

With that said of all the people in my life I need to thank Bryan. He's been there through some of my darkest moments and helped me find my light again. He's stepped in like Ben did for Anthony, but also so much more than that. I've always loved stories for how they bring the impossible to life, but every day with you is another day where you show me that the impossible can be possible in the real world too. You help me see the love, magic and adventure that can happen in the every day life.

To my tiny humans who are coming on that journey with me, enjoying some of the wonderful adventures we go on and who are not so tiny any more at all.

To Bear, Andrew and David, yet again. You three form the majority of what I have left in my life and one day soon I hope to repay you all for the support and unwavering friendship you've shown. The next round is definitely on me.

And not the least thank you at all, to LMBPN and especially Robin. You've been one of my favorite people in the world for a while now and with you and all the other awesome people at LMBPN working on my stories, I know that they're in good hands. You are family and I hope that we're always working on something together.

And finally to God. For never giving up.

ABOUT THE AUTHOR

Jess is in the process of changing her name. She's been through a difficult year that leaves her wanting a fresh start and a chance to be the person she's always meant to be. Over the next little while all her books will be moving to Talia Beckett and you'll find all future releases under this author name.

Talia was born in the quaint village of Woodbridge in the UK, has spent some of her childhood in the States and now resides near the beautiful Roman city of Bath. She lives with her two tiny humans (one boy and one girl) and near an amazing group of friends who support her career and life choices.

During her still relatively short life Talia has displayed an innate curiosity for learning new things and has therefore studied many subjects, from maths and the sciences, to history and drama. Talia now works full time as a writer and mummy, incorporating many of the subjects she has an interest in within her plots and characters.

When she's not busy with work and keeping her tiny humans alive she can often be found with friends, playing with miniature characters, dice and pieces of paper covered in funny stats and notes about fictional adventures her figures have been on.

You can find out more about the author and her

upcoming projects by joining her on facebook, by watching her live D&D streams, or emailing her via books@jessmountifield.co.uk. Talia loves hearing from a happy fan so please do get in touch!

Talia is also opening up her discord for fans to come chat about what she's up to, and see a few sneak peaks of future work. There's also a chance to become one of her beta readers. If you'd like to check that out you can do so here.

CONNECT WITH THE AUTHOR

Connect with Talia

Mailing list sign up
Facebook group.
Discord group
Actual play D&D stream: Twitch or Youtube
Email address: contact me here.

BOOKS BY JESS MOUNTIFIELD / TALIA BECKETT

Already published

Urban Fantasy

Dragon of Shadow and Air:

Air Bound

Shadow Sworn

Dragon Souled

Earth Bound

Night Sworn

Dryad Souled

Water Bound

Day Sworn

Pegasus Souled

Fire Bound

Light Sworn

Phoenix Souled

Dragon Apparent:

Dragon Missing

Dragon Seeking

Time of the Dragon (with Andrew Bellingham):

Dragon's Code
Dragon's Inquisition

Fantasy

Tales of Ethanar:

Wandering to Belong (Tale 1)

Innocent Hearts (Tale 2 & 3)

For Such a Time as This (Tale 4)

A Fire's Sacrifice (Tale 5)

Winter Series:

The Hope of Winter (Tale 6.05)

The Fire of Winter (Tale 6.1)

Guild of the Eternal Flame:

Wayfarer's Sanctuary

Protector's Secret

Healer's Oath

Other Fantasy:

The Initiate (under Holly Lujah)

Writing with Dawn Chapman:

Jessica's Challenge (#5 in the Puatera Online series)

Dahlia's Shadow (#6 in the Puatera Online series)

Lila's Revenge (#7 in the Puatera Online series)

Sci-Fi:

Fringe Colonies:

Alliance

Haven

Rebellion

Rebirth

Reclamation

Star Trail:

Hunted

Sherdan series:

Sherdan's Prophecy

Sherdan's Legacy

Sherdan's Country

Sherdan's Road (A short story in the anthology 'The End of the Road')

The Slave Who'd Never Been Kissed (A short in the charity anthology 'Imaginings')

New Beginnings

Santa's Little Space Pirate

In the multi-author Adamanta series:

Episode 1 – Adamanta

Episode 3 – Excelsior

Episode 8 – Phoenix

Episode 13 – New Contacts

Episode 17 – Sacrifice

Other:

Clues, Claws and Christmas

Non-Fic:

How to Write Lots, and Get Sh*t Done: the Art of Not Being a Flake

Find purchase links here

Coming soon:

Urban Fantasy:

Dragon Apparent:

Dragon Revealed

Dragon Rising

Dragon Defying

Dragon Crowned

Time of the Dragon (with Andrew Bellingham):

Dragon's Redemption

Dragon's Revolt

Fantasy:

(Tales of Ethanar):

The Pursuit of Winter (#2 in the Winter series, Tale 6.2)

Books under Amelia Price

Mycroft Holmes Adventures:

The Hundred Year Wait

The Unexpected Coincidence

The Invisible Amateur

The Female Charm

The Reluctant Knight

The Ambitious Orphan

The Unconventional Honeymoon Gift

The Family Reunion

The Immortal Problem

The Unremarkable Assistant

Coming soon:

Mycroft 11

OTHER BOOKS FROM LMBPN PUBLISHING

Sign up for the LMBPN email list to be notified of new releases and special deals!

https://lmbpn.com/email/

For a complete list of books by LMBPN please visit:

https://lmbpn.com/books-by-lmbpn-publishing/

www.ingramcontent.com/pod-product-compliance
Lightning Source LLC
LaVergne TN
LVHW091717070526
838199LV00050B/2428